D1009800

Advance Praise for
Chicano Chicanery

"A fine debut collection. Chacón has the sensibility (and sense of humor!) to bring these stories heartbreakingly to life."
—Cristina Garcia, author of
Dreaming in Cuban and *The Agüero Sisters*

"These stories make you think, and they reach the heart with a cast of unique characters and surprise endings. An outstanding collection."
—Rudolfo Anaya, author of
Bless Me Ultima and the Sonny Baca mystery series

CHICANO CHICANERY

Short Stories

by

Daniel Chacón

Arte Público Press
Houston, Texas
2000

This volume is made possible through grants from the National Endowment for the Arts (a federal agency), Andrew W. Mellon Foundation, the Lila Wallace-Reader's Digest Fund and the City of Houston through The Cultural Arts Council of Houston, Harris County.

Recovering the past, creating the future

Arte Público Press
University of Houston
Houston, Texas 77204-2174

Chacón, Daniel.
    Chicano chicanery : short stories / by Daniel Chacón.
    p.   cm.
    Contents: Andy the office boy — Godoy lives — The biggest city in the world — Ofrenda — Expression of our people — Aztlán, Oregon — Mexican table — Spring break — Torture fantasy — Slow and good — How hot was Mexicali? — Too white — Story #7 in D minor.
    ISBN 1-55885-280-8 (pbk. : alk. paper)
    1. United States — Social life and customs — 20th century — Fiction. 2. Mexico — Social life and customs — 20th century — Fiction 3. Mexican Americans — Social life and customs — Fiction. I. Title.
    PS3553.H215 C47   2000
    813'.54—dc21   00-020792

♾ The paper used in this publication meets the requirements of the American National Standard for Information Sciences—Permanence of Paper for Printed Library Materials, ANSI Z39.48-1984.

Stories in this book appeared in different form in the following journals: "Expression of Our People," *The New England Review;* "Aztlán, Oregon," *The Americas Review* and *The Floating Borderlands: 25 Years of U.S. Hispanic Literature;* "Spring Break," *The Bilingual Review;* "Godoy Lives," *The Clakamas Review;* "Ofrenda," *Colorado Review;* "Mexican Table," *in the grove* and *RiverSedge.*

© 2000 by Daniel Chacón
Printed in the United States of America

HOUSTON PUBLIC LIBRARY

R01155 93267

10 9 8 7 6 5 4 3 2 1

In memory of
Lucinda Chacón
1940-1989

I tried to love once
but ended up punching
everyone.

—*Andrés Montoya*

Contents

Andy the Office Boy

All the lawyers agreed, Andy's loyalty should be richly rewarded in the form of a Christmas gift. They chose Rachel Garcia, the youngest and newest of the attorneys, a recent Harvard graduate, to take up the collection. Carrying a cigar box around the floors of the firm, she managed to get fifty dollars from each of the partners, twenty-five each from the attorneys, and ten dollars each from the paralegals and secretaries, so after a week of soliciting, she had collected $780. No one knew how much she had collected, nor did they care what she got him—"Something nice," they told her— so, embittered for being asked to do such a menial job, after having graduated at the top of her class, she walked to the parking garage in the drizzling snow, pulling her coat over her face like a vampire, tempted to suck a commission from the total. Perhaps, she thought, her black eyes glittering with ideas, she should spend a hundred bucks on a nice dinner, a bottle of red wine, a seafood appetizer. Guilt, however, reminded her of Andy.

He was a skinny blonde boy with a degree in English from SSU in southern Minnesota. He would walk into her office after knocking lightly on the doorframe, carrying a bag heavy with her deli order, which he had run across the street to get for her, and he refused to keep the change. He always brought his own lunch to work, peanut butter and jelly and a Snickers bar. He never ate downtown, because, he always said, Who can afford to eat out on an office boy's salary? She remembered how he had told her, with bright blue eyes, how he had wanted to go to Boston to be a bartender in a sports bar—just like Sam Malone—but he only made it as far as Minneapolis because his ex-

1

girlfriend got pregnant and a court ordered that he support the kid.

The cold night air stung Rachel's face. She felt the $780 in her pocket, not as if it were heavy, but as if it were a warm throb inside her jacket, like a living heart.

She walked along the Nicolette Mall, the windows displaying expensive winter coats and boots and sweaters. On her salary, 43K, she couldn't buy nice things, not because it was bad starting pay for a recent graduate, or poor pay for a single girl living in the Twin Cities, but because she lived in a condo with parking in uptown and she drove a new SUV. Plus, she paid three hundred dollars a month in student loans, so that after all her checks were written, she felt like a pauper, as if she were still in law school. The feeling that she should spend some of Andy's gift money, something, anything, made her hungry to spend it.

Who was that boy anyway and why did the lawyers like him so much? He had a kind of sickly smile, like he was dying of cancer, and his eyes darted about as if they were too eager to land on one spot. Quite frankly, he spent much of his workday at the secretary's desk e-mailing friends and family, or trying to flirt with the file clerks who pushed carts in and out of offices handing out manila folders, girls barely eighteen, with thin hips and eyes fat with ambition. They always said, "No, Andy," without even looking at him.

Why did the lawyers like him so much? Maybe simply because he was Andy the office boy, and after two years with the firm, it was clear that he wanted no more out of life than being Andy the office boy, no more dreams of bartending in Boston, no thoughts of graduate school or becoming a professional in any field. He was the one person in the firm, perhaps the one person she now knew—having been at Harvard the last three years—who wanted nothing more than to wake up every morning being who he was and doing what he would do that day. He was not a simpleton, but he was simple.

Was it a good idea, she thought, walking into the warm belly of the City Center Mall, to give such a humble boy a $780 gift? The possibility that it could corrupt him, that it could remind him that there was a material world, could take away a quality about him, something she liked to refer to as Euro-American noble savagery. He was, to her, the essence of rural Minnesota. As the junior member of the firm, she performed the unwanted duty of driving south of the Cities into the prairie, to do research with clients in towns like Gibbon and Gaylord and Renville, and one time she stopped in Marshall, Andy's hometown, where she walked into the Wooden Nickel for dinner, a pub packed with people she was sure were Andy's relatives and friends, thick Norwegians and Germans drinking beer and eating popcorn. So many of those blue eyes strained to see through the sunlight, to see her standing in the open door, a Chicana with a briefcase.

She tried on sweaters and skirts and pants and coats and about twenty pairs of shoes, longing to buy something, just one thing with the money meant for him. Her clothes, although professional and smart looking, had fading fringes. She had only gotten a few paychecks so far, and she had no savings and her three credit cards had been maxed out in law school. Her parents were no help because together they made far less than what she made. They still rented an apartment on a dark, narrow street in downtown El Paso. She didn't dare tell them how much she earned because they would think it was a lot and might expect her to send money home.

In Saks Fifth Avenue, she tried on a baby-blue cashmere sweater, so soft on her flesh that it seemed like a feather massage. She saw herself wearing that sweater, walking the offices of the firm with confidence and power and the knowledge that people were noticing her. It cost $550. She handed it to the salesgirl and said, "No, thank you."

The snow let up and she walked downtown for several blocks. She passed cafes, bars, jazz clubs, and nice restaurants, all of them full of happy people. What she saw next stopped her walk. It was a three-story brick building with a bright red neon sign hanging down the side. "Sex World."

She had been so focused on law school and now on work that she let no one near her, and, not being good at casual sex, she had gone without it for almost four years. Seeing the flashing lights of Sex World, desire gnawed at her, not because she felt stimulated by pornography—she felt it demeaning and exploitative and ugly—but because the letters *s.e.x.* and the concrete action that those letters represented caused her to feel the full weight of her loneliness.

She entered Sex World, relieved to see couples and young women among the shoppers. The first floor had videos fitting most fetishes, and there were peep shows in the back. She was looking at the video boxes when she heard a familiar whine. It was Andy the office boy, saying to the clerk, "More change. More change." She furtively followed him and saw him go into a booth. The young lawyer heard the door lock. Then she heard him say, "Yes. Nice. Nice."

When the day came to give Andy his gift, all the lawyers gathered in the main office and said, "Surprise!" as the office boy walked in. He smiled broadly and waved at everybody. Everyone turned to Rachel Garcia. One lawyer said, "The gift."

The young lawyer cleared her throat. "Andy," she said, "this is from all of us. We collected money from everyone and got you this."

"Show it," they said. "Let him have it."

"But," she said, "it's too big to drag around. So come with me. They all know what it is," she said, and the lawyers agreed, because it would seem insensitive to not know what they had gotten him.

"We'll be right back," she said.

And everybody said, "Of course," as if they had arranged it that way.

She led him into the conference room. "Sit down," she said. He nervously sat. To Andy's astonishment, the pretty lawyer undid the buttons of her baby-blue cashmere sweater.

"Oh," he said, watching her pull it down her smooth, dark shoulders. "Nice. Very nice," he said.

Godoy Lives

Juan's cousin wrote what he knew of the dead guy. He was from Jalisco. Not married. Some called him *maricón* because they suspected he was gay, but no one knew for sure.

The age of the man was the same as Juan's, 24, and the picture on the green card strikingly similar, sunken cheeks, small forehead, tiny, deep-set eyes that on Juan looked as if everything scared him, but that on the dead guy looked focused, confident. "You could use this to come work here," his cousin wrote.

It was perfect, Juan thought, if not for the name written on the green card: Miguel Valencia Godoy.

Godoy? Juan wasn't even sure how to pronounce it. His wife Maria held the green card in her small, work-gnarled hand and she looked at the name, then at Juan.

"Goo doy," she said.

He tried: "Guld Yoy."

Patiently, she took a breath. "Goo doy."

He practiced and practiced. It got so the entire family was saying it: Maria, their four-year-old boy Juan Jr., and even the big-eyed baby girl came close with "goo goo." Only Juan couldn't say it. Some nights Maria kept him up late, pushing him awake as he dozed off, until he said it correctly three times in a row.

When the day came for him to leave, he kissed her goodbye, shook his son's hand like a man, and kissed the baby's soft, warm head. The treeless dirt road stretched into the barren hills, reaching toward the nearest town seven miles away where he would catch the bus to Tijuana.

"I'll be back," he said to Maria.

"I know you will," she said.

"I'll send money when I find work."

"I know you will," she said. She placed an open palm on his face. "You're a good man, Juan. I know you'll do what's right."

He looked into her eyes, disappointed that he could not find in them a single tear. She smiled sadly, like a mother sending her child off to school.

"Go, Juan," she said. "Don't make this harder than it needs to be."

"I can't help it." He wept. She hugged him in her strong, bony arms. She smelled of body odor. "Don't do this. Be a man," she said firmly.

He pulled away from her, wiped his tears, and said, "I'm going."

"Again," she said.

"Duld Woy," he sniveled.

"Goo doy. Again."

"Goose boy."

"Juan, if you don't get it, things will be bad."

At the border, he nervously stepped across a red line painted on the sidewalk. He stepped past warning signs that ordered people to turn back if not able to enter the U. S. Inside the building, big and bright as an indoor sports stadium, he was surprised at the number of Mexicans waiting in line to get to the U. S. side. Still, most of the people were white, holding bags of souvenirs, colorful Mexican blankets, ceramics, bottles of tequila. He looked at the heads of the lines to see which U. S. immigration officer he should approach.

People who knew had told him that the worst immigration officers in the U.S. were the ones of Mexican descent. Pick a white officer, he had heard, because the Mexican-American, the Chicano INS officers had to prove to the white people that they were no longer Mexicans. He had heard in the mountains that they would beat people up or sic vicious dogs on them, laughing as the bloody flesh would fly in all directions.

There were three open lines, three officers, a white woman, and two white men. He chose a young man with a shaved head whose line moved fast because he barely looked at the IDs held out to him, just waved everyone through, bored, like he didn't want to be there.

Juan knew that this would be easier than he had imagined. With a confidence he had never felt before, he said to himself, slightly out loud, in perfect pronunciation, "Godoy."

When he was two people from the front, something terrible happened. A tall Chicano officer tapped the white agent on the shoulder and said something. The white guy smiled, stood up, and left, leaving the tall Chicano to take his place. This Mexican American was mean-looking, well over six feet tall, with massive shoulders and legs thick as tree trunks. His green INS uniform stretched like a football player's. Set below his flat forehead, above his chubby cheeks, were small black eyes that darted suspiciously from face to face. His hair was cut short to his head, sticking straight up, and he didn't smile.

Juan wanted to get out of the line, but he was next.

The Chicano looked down at him. "Why should I let you through?" he demanded in English.

Juan didn't understand a word except for "you," which he believed meant him, but he assumed the officer had asked for his green card, so he held it up.

And smiled.

The Chicano looked suspiciously into Juan's eyes. He grabbed the card from his fingers and looked closely at the picture, then back at Juan.

"What's your name?" he asked in Spanish.

Juan took a deep breath and said, "Miguel Valencia Goo Poo."

"What?" asked the officer, chest inflating with air.

Juan was sure he'd be grabbed by the collar and dragged out.

He tried again: "Miguel Valencia Godoy."

"What's that last name?"

Sweat trickled down his back.

"Godoy?" he offered.

"Where are you from?"

"Jalisco," he remembered.

The officer put the ID card on the counter and said, with a big smile, "Cousin! It's me!"

He had said it in Spanish, but the words still had no meaning to Juan.

"I'm your cousin. Francisco Pancho Montes Godoy."

"Oh?"

"Don't you remember me?"

"Oh, Pancho, of course," said Juan, weakly.

"You lying son of a bitch," said Pancho. "You don't even recognize me. Come on," he said, coming around the counter. "I know what to do with guys like you." He picked up the duffel bag as effortlessly as if it were a purse, and led Juan across the vast floor of the building, through crowds of people, into a little room with chairs, a TV, and magazines in English. Pancho dropped the bag, turned around and said *"Un abrazo,"* holding out his long and thick arms. He hugged the breath out of Juan. He smelled of freshly cleaned laundry. Then he held him at arm's length to get a better look.

"You haven't changed. You wait right here. When I get off, I'm taking you home. You can see my wife and kids." He started to walk out, but something struck him. He turned around. "Oh, I just thought of something."

"What?"

"Really. It just occurred to me."

"What did?"

"I have a special surprise for you, Miguel."

"What surprise?" asked Juan.

"You'll see," said Pancho. "A surprise."

Juan waited about three hours in that room. One time he tried to escape, but when he opened the door, Pancho, from behind the counter, looked right at him and winked.

At last, Pancho opened the door. He was now dressed in street clothes, 501 jeans and a T-shirt with a faded image of Mickey Mouse. He looked like a giant kid.

"Come on, cousin," he said. "I'm taking you home."

Like a lamb led to the slaughter, Juan followed through the parking lot, looking between the rows for an escape route, Pancho's shadow stretching across the hoods of several cars. Pancho grabbed him by the arm with a strong grip and escorted him to the passenger's side of an over-sized Ford pickup. Juan pictured Maria wearing a black dress and veil, standing over his grave, not weeping, just shaking her head, saying, "Dumb Juan. Why can't he do nothing right?"

He climbed up into the cab, using both hands and feet, like a child climbing a tree. He had to get out of there quick, find his real cousin, the one who had sent him the dead man's green card, and work his ass off so he could send Maria money. She needed him. His family needed him.

They drove through town, the truck so high off the ground Juan thought that surely this must be what it was like to be on a horse. He held on to the rim of the seat.

"Hey, cousin. Listen to me," Pancho said. "You'll never guess the surprise I have for you."

"What is it?" Juan asked.

Pancho laughed an evil laugh.

"You'll see," he said.

"Can you give me a hint?"

"You won't be disappointed. So, tell me, where have you been these last years?"

"I'm not married," Juan said, remembering another detail about Godoy.

"Oh?" Pancho asked.

"Never found someone I loved," he said.

" Well, here you'll find plenty of women. Lorena has a pretty sister. Lorena turned out to be the greatest wife in the world."

Juan wanted to say, no, that Maria was the greatest, but he couldn't.

He had seen her at an outdoor dance in the *zócalo* of a nearby town one sunny Sunday afternoon. She was the prettiest girl there, wearing a white dress that fell just above her knees, her cinnamon-colored legs smooth and shapely. She was seventeen. All afternoon guys stood around her like giants, boys with large shoulders, black cowboy boots, and white straw cowboy hats that shined in the sun, while Juan, a skinny, sickly looking boy barely eighteen, watched her from behind the balloon vendor. Still, Maria noticed him.

As was the custom, the unmarried young people walked in a circle at the center of the plaza, girls in one direction, boys in another, and although several girls were available, most of the boys eyed

Maria, and when they passed her, they threw confetti in her long black hair, or they offered their hands to her, but she walked by each of them, looking at Juan the entire time. He, in turn, looked over his shoulder at the tiled dome of the cathedral, convinced she was looking past him. Since she was rejecting so many others, he decided it wouldn't be so bad when she rejected him, so he was determined to throw some confetti in her hair. When she was right beside him, he raised his clenched hand, but when he opened it, he realized he had nothing. *What a fool I am!* he cried to himself. But Maria brushed out the confetti already in her hair and offered him her hand. So excited, he wasn't sure with which hand to take hers, extending one, withdrawing it, extending the other, so she took control. She grabbed his arm and led him away from the circle.

Pancho pulled the truck into a gravel lot lined by a three-foot-tall chain-link fence that surrounded a large front yard and a small house. Two dogs barked at the truck, a German shepherd and a big black lab. "Here we are, *primo*," he said. "This is home."

Pancho opened the fence and the dogs jumped on him for affection, but then they stopped and seemed to wait for Juan to enter the yard, their tongues hanging out, tails wagging, whining as if unable to contain their excitement.

"Do they bite?" Juan asked.

"Don't worry, they only bite strangers," said Pancho.

"That's good," Juan said. The dogs surrounded him, sniffing his crotch, his legs, the Michoacán dirt caked to his boots.

The men entered the house, which had purple shag carpet and a velveteen couch and love seat. The painting above the TV was a velvet likeness of the Aztec warrior with the dead woman in his arms. The place smelled of beans cooking.

"Lorena," called Pancho. "He's here." Then he looked at Juan. "I called her and told her you'd be coming."

Lorena, a strikingly handsome woman in a jean skirt, which came above her knees, and a white T-shirt that hugged her voluptuous body, walked in, wiping her hands on a dish towel. Standing next to each other, she and her husband looked like the perfect couple, him tall and broad-shouldered, a little chubby around the middle and on the face, and her, tall, big boned, wide hips. She had a long jaw like an Indian and long black hair tied in a ponytail.

"I don't believe it," she said. She ran up and gave Juan a big hug. Her flesh was soft and pillowy, and she smelled of fresh onions. She held him at arm's length. "This is such a wonderful day. Imagine," she said. "Just imagine."

"Imagine," Pancho said, his hands on his hips, smiling big.

Juan wasn't sure if Godoy had ever met Lorena, so he wasn't sure what to say. He said, "Imagine."

"I have your room ready for you," she said. "Do you want to wash up or rest?"

"Later," said Pancho. "First he has to meet the girls."

He led Juan down the hallway. Framed family pictures lined the walls. At one metal frame with multiple photos, Pancho stopped and pointed to two little kids dressed like cowboys, holding toy guns and trying to look mean. "You remember that?"

It was Pancho and the dead man as kids. Juan looked closely. The similarities between that child and how he remembered looking as a child were so great that it spooked him, as if he had had two lives that went on simultaneously. He almost remembered that day playing cowboys.

"That was in Jalisco," Juan said.

"That's right. On grandfather's ranch. Remember that ranch?"

Juan pictured acres of land, a stable with twenty of the finest horses, and a garden where the family ate dinner, served by Indians, on a long wooden table. "Do I," he said dreamily.

"And all those horses," Pancho said, sadly delighted. "Oh, well, come on. We have plenty of time to reminisce, but first I want you to meet the girls."

Juan expected that he was referring to Lorena's sisters, but when Pancho opened a bedroom door, two little girls, five-year-old black-eyed twins, sat on the floor playing with dolls. They looked up at their father. "Hello, daddy," they said in unison.

"Come here, sweethearts. I want you to meet someone."

Obediently they rose and came to their father, standing on either side of him. "This is your *Tío* Miguel."

Both girls ran to Juan and hugged him. "Hi, *tío*. We love you."

They smelled of baby powder.

Lorena insisted he go to bed early because of his long journey, so after dinner—chile verde with fat flour tortillas—she led him into the extra bedroom and clicked on a table lamp, an arc of light appearing like a holy apparition across the white wall. Their shadows were so tall that their heads touched the ceiling. She showed him the shower and where they kept the towels. When she bent over to explain how to use the stereo, her T-shirt hung open, exposing her cleavage. She slowly kissed him on the forehead, soft, wet lips, and she left him alone. As he lay in bed he felt himself aroused. As much as he tried to picture Maria, he couldn't stop seeing Lorena, nor could he help but fantasize about what her sister looked like. He reached in his underwear and felt for himself, but on the high part of the wall, above the shadow of his horizontal body, in the arc of light, he saw an image of Maria as if wearing a veil. He turned off the lamp.

The next day Pancho woke him early and said it was his day off and he'd show Juan around.

"And tomorrow I'm calling in sick. We have so much to do."

As they drove through the city, Juan said, "I need to work, *primo*. I need a job."

"What are you going to do?" said Pancho.

"I have some connections in Fresno," said Juan. "I thought I'd go there and pick fruit."

Pancho laughed. "That's wetback work."

I *am* a wetback, Juan thought. But he said, "I'm not experienced enough at anything else."

"Miguel. Miguelito," said Pancho, shaking his head. His chubby cheeks were slightly pockmarked from acne as a teenager. "I got it all figured out, *primo*. Don't worry."

They drove out of town onto a narrow, two-lane highway lined by tall pine trees, until they reached a clearing, a vast green ranch set in a glen, beyond which the ocean lay over the horizon like a sparkling blue sheet. They entered a white gate with the name of the ranch, Cielito Lindo, and drove on the paved driveway until they reached a three-story Spanish style hacienda.

"What is this place?" Juan asked.

"You'll see."

A white man in his fifties walked out of the mansion. He wore tight jeans and a flannel shirt tucked in and was in good shape for his age. His gray hair was balding on the top. He smiled as he approached Juan, extending his hand. "Welcome, Miguel. My name's BD. Pancho told me all about you and the funny thing that happened at the border." Although he spoke with an American accent, he spoke Spanish well.

"Yes, it was very funny," Juan said.

"What are the chances?" BD said.

BD led them around the mansion to the stables, white wooden buildings with so many doors extending on the horizon that it looked like a mirror image of itself. People led horses in and out of the doors. They entered one and saw horses proudly standing in their stalls, white and black Arabians, their nostrils flaring as if aware of their own worth. A Mexican man was brushing one of them, and as he stroked her silky neck, he cooed how beautiful she was.

"Memo," BD said to the man.

Memo looked up.

"This is Miguel Godoy. He's going to join our team."

"It's very nice to meet you," said Juan.

"Guillermo Reyes." the man said, extending his hand to Juan. "Godoy you say? Is that a Mexican name?"

"Of course it is," said Juan.

"Well, the name itself isn't," said Pancho. "But our family is pure Mexican. Although we're the first generation of American," he said, proudly putting his arm around Juan.

Memo's eyes scrutinized Juan. "Are you from Michoacán?"

"No, hell no. He's from Jalisco," said Pancho, offended by the thought.

"You sound like you're from Michoacán," Memo said.

Over iced tea under a white gazebo, BD explained how he became part owner of the ranch when he was Pancho's age, twenty-five, and he had invested money in the land with four other partners. Over the years they built the country club, the stables, and bought twenty more acres on which their customers rode the horses. Some of the horses they took care of for the rich and famous. BD, who worked as an INS officer with Pancho, would retire in a few years a rich man. "I'll spend all my time out here."

"See, cousin, that's the secret of success. You spend your lifetime investing. Right now I'm thinking about buying into an apartment building. We'll invest our money together, cousin, and we'll be rich."

"What money?" Juan asked.

"What money," Pancho repeated, laughing.

Juan's job at the ranch, BD explained, was to take the horses out of the stable for the customers, make sure the customers mounted safely, and then return the horses to Memo or another stable hand when the ride was over.

"But I don't speak English," Juan said.

"What a great way to learn," Pancho said.

"I don't know anything about horses," Juan said.

"He's being modest," Pancho said. "He has a gift."

When BD told Juan how much he'd be earning, Juan had to hear it again to be certain he had heard right.

"And the best part of it is," said Pancho, "Tax free. Cash."

That evening Lorena's sister, Elida, an eighteen-year-old with light brown hair and golden eyes, had dinner with the family. She was so beautiful that Juan couldn't stop sneaking looks at her, and she frequently looked at him and smiled shyly, which made the little black-eyed twins put their tiny hands over their mouths and giggle. When Pancho broke out with the stories about Miguel as a child, how brave he was and how everyone knew he'd be a great man, how girls used to follow him around, about the fights he'd get into with older and bigger boys, Elida looked at him with a stare that bordered on awe. Juan relished the stories, picturing it all and almost believing that he had done those things. After dinner, while the family was drinking coffee and the little girls were eating their dessert, Juan stood up and said he'd like to get some fresh air. He looked at Elida and asked if she would join him.

She said she'd love to.

On the patio they sat on the swing. The full moon shone like a cross in the black sky and reflected in Elida's large eyes. Her face was smooth. The sweet smell of her perfume rose like curls of smoke and swam into his nose, reaching so far into him that they massaged his heart. "Can I touch your face?" he said.

"My face? That's funny. Why for would you want to do that?"

Her Spanish wasn't good, but she had probably never been to Mexico.

"Because it's the most beautiful face I have ever seen."

She lowered her eyes. He kept looking at the smoothness of her skin, down her thin neck—a birthmark at the protruding bone. Her breasts.

"Okay," she said. "You can touch."

He looked up.

He reached out his hand, opened his palm, and as if he were touching something sacred, he slowly felt the warmth of her face. Passionately, she pressed her cheek into his hand and she closed her eyes and sighed. "That's nice," she said, opening her eyes and looking into his.

Lorena called them inside to watch a movie they had rented. Side by side on the love seat, they glanced as often at each other as they did at the TV. When it was over, Elida said she had to get home. Juan walked her to the car. She opened the door, but before she got in she turned around, bit her bottom lip, and peered at him with eyes that spoke of desire. "I guess I'll see you later," she said.

"You will."

He watched her pull onto the street, her taillights disappearing into the darkness.

When he went back into the house, Pancho and Lorena were waiting for him, standing side by side, big smiles on their faces.

Although it hadn't been two days, these two seemed so familiar, so much like family. It occurred to him that he could keep this up for a long time, maybe forever. Maybe they would never know. Juan, quite frankly, was having a good time.

What was the rush to work in those hot fields, making less in one month than what he'd make in a week at the stables? He could still send Maria money.

Maria.

She hadn't even cried when he left. She was probably glad he was gone.

"Well, cousin, tell us," Pancho said, as if he couldn't stand the anticipation. "What did you think of Lorena's sister?"

Juan laughed, heading toward the hallway to his bedroom, and he said, as if the question carried its own answer, "What did I think of Lorena's sister."

Life was great.

He made plenty of money, much of which he spent taking Elida to restaurants. He was beginning to learn English, and Pancho wanted them to invest in real estate together, as a team. When Juan reminded him he didn't have much money, Pancho assured him it would work out. "I don't think that'll be a problem," he said. One day at work, feeling good after a night with Elida, wherein they went further than they ever had, although not all the way, he was friendly and joked with the customers in English. Around midday, he got this urge to have lunch with someone, to click glasses with an old friend. In the stables he searched for Memo but couldn't find him, not in the country club or walking around the grounds. Finally, as he was walking around the back of the stables, he saw him at a picnic table, eating lunch with his family, his wife and two kids, a little boy and a little girl. They weren't talking as they ate, but it was a such a picture of happiness that for the first time in a long time, he thought of his own kids, Juan Jr., the baby, and he felt a great loss for his Maria.

What was she going to do without him? The right thing to do would be to take the money he had already earned, perhaps earn a little more, and send it to Maria. Wherever she was at that moment, whatever she was doing, there was no doubt in her mind that he was going to come back. He had to quit seeing Elida.

Later that night they were walking along the pier in San Diego when he decided to tell her it was over between them. He said, "I think you should know something."

Elida stopped walking and looked at him. Her eyes filled with love and hope. Anticipation.

"I love you," he blurted.

They kissed.

Later that night in her small bedroom plastered with glossy Ricky Martin posters, they made love. Her parents were out of town.

Afterwards, as he held her smooth body in his thin arms, the smell of her perfume mixed with the scent of the peach candle flickering on her nightstand, he told her that he never wanted to be without her. And he meant it. He was in love.

When he got home, Pancho was sitting on the couch waiting for him, his big legs crossed, his arm extended across the back of the sofa.

"What's up?" Juan asked.

"Remember that surprise I told you about?"

"What surprise?" asked Juan.

"When I first saw you at the border. I told you I had a surprise for you."

"Oh yeah," said Juan.

"Well, tomorrow I'm going to let you have it," he said, standing up.

When Juan woke up the next morning, Pancho had already left. He found Lorena in the kitchen cutting a melon into bite-sized slices. She told him that Pancho went to get the surprise. As she served him a plate of the melon and a cup of strong, black coffee, she saw the concern in his face. "Don't worry so much," she said as she sat at the table opposite him.

He remained silent, worried.

"You do like it here with me and Pancho, right?"

He was distracted, but he still said yes.

"Look," she said, feeling sorry for him, "I think what Pancho's doing is wrong. I told him so. If you're not prepared for it, things could be difficult."

"What are you talking about?"

"The surprise. I told him not to do it this way, but he wouldn't listen. Sometimes he doesn't think things out fully. This is one of those times."

"What's the surprise?" asked Juan.

"Okay, I'm going to tell you," Lorena said. "But only because I don't think it's right what he's doing."

Pancho went to the Greyhound bus station, she said, to pick up Godoy's mother who had been living in El Paso. He was bringing her here so she could live with Miguel, her only living son.

The world fell on him. It was over. A mother would always know who her son was. "Don't worry," said Lorena. "She'll be so happy to see you. She never stopped being your mother."

After eating a couple of pieces of melon and drinking coffee, Juan said he wasn't feeling well and wanted to lie down. When he got into his bedroom, he quickly pulled the dirty duffel bag from the closet and started packing everything that would fit. He grabbed the cash he had already earned and stuffed it at the very bottom of his socks and then pulled on his boots. He had to be gone before Pancho got back. He would lose out on a few days pay, but better that than lose his life. He was ready to go, when he heard a knock on the bedroom door. He stuffed the bag in the closet and jumped into bed, pulling the covers over his body. "Come in," he said.

Lorena walked in, disturbed. She pulled the chair that was leaning against the wall and scooted it close to the bed. "There's something else. And this is it. I mean this is really it. This is why I'm telling you what Pancho's doing. I think you need to be prepared."

"What?" he said.

"It's been a long time since you've seen her." She paused, as if the words were too difficult. "Miguel, your mother is getting very senile."

"How senile?" he said, perking up.

"She forgets things sometimes. People sometimes. And . . ."

"What? What?"

"After your father disowned you—and she still doesn't believe the story."

"The story?"

"About you and that other boy. She doesn't believe it. None of us do."

"Uh, that's good."

"But after he disowned you, she never gave up on you. She knew she would see you again. She's been saving things for you. After your father died, he left, well, quite a bit of money."

"How much?"

"A lot, Miguel. You don't even have to work if you don't want. She's been saving it for you. I only tell you this because I want you to be prepared. I told Pancho it wasn't a good idea to not tell you first. But he was just so excited about the, you know, the . . . Well, he wants you to be happy."

"What if she doesn't recognize me?" he asked.

"She's senile. It just means we'd have to . . . What am I saying? She will."

Juan sat up on his bed. "Well, then, I'll look forward to meeting her. I mean, seeing her again."

Lorena left the room. Juan paced back and forth with a burst of energy. When he heard the truck pull up onto the gravel, he said to himself, "Here we go." He looked at himself in the mirror. He saw staring at him Miguel Valencia Godoy. Clean-shaven, handsome, lean-bodied, confident. But then he glimpsed something that bothered him, a dull gleam in his eyes, something that didn't belong to him. Insecurity. It was Juan. He shook it off and went out into the living room to see his mother.

The Biggest City
in the World

Harvey Gomez stepped off the plane in Mexico City and couldn't believe what he saw: Among the multitudes of *mestizos* walking through the airport was Professor David P. Rogstart, followed by a little Mexican boy carrying his luggage. Gomez quickly showed his papers to the Mexican official and ran through the crowd to catch the professor. When he got close enough to where he could see the familiar red-orange shine of Rogstart's bald head, he yelled, "Professor Rogstart! Professor Rogstart!"

The professor, at least a foot taller than almost everyone else in the airport, turned around, not as if surprised to hear his name, but with impatience, as if to say, "What do you want now?"

Gomez jumped on his toes as he walked, trying to show himself above the heads of the Mexicans. He raised his hands and yelled, "Here, Professor, here!"

Gomez tried to move faster, but the crowd was too dense. Then a little Indian woman, even shorter than him, stood right in front of him with sad eyes, a wrinkled face, and an empty palm extended for alms. *"Por favor, joven, regálame un taco."*

"Yeah, right," he said to himself as he twisted around her like a matador. Finally, he reached the professor.

"Professor, it's me!"

Rogstart stopped and looked around, but his gaze was high, so Gomez, feeling a little silly, had to raise his arm, as if to say, "I'm

21

down here."

"Oh, hello, Harvey," the professor said, as if running into him were something ordinary.

But Gomez didn't think it was ordinary, so he spilled out his words like a child: "Imagine you and I seeing each other in the world's biggest city! How weird! Isn't that the weirdest thing in the world?"

"Actually, no," said the professor, quite calmly. "In fact, it makes a lot of sense that we would run into each other."

"How's that?"

The professor, removing the specs from his pale blue eyes, spoke with a hint of impatience, like professors sound when asked questions that have already been answered. "You're a graduate student," he said, "who studies Mexico. I'm a professor and scholar of Mexican history. It's winter vacation, so we have a month off. This is an historically important city. In fact, the only thing that might surprise me is that we weren't on the same flight."

"But Mexico City's the biggest city in the world!"

"It makes complete sense," Rogstart said, the subject closed.

A Mexican man in rags came up and asked something of the professor, but he spoke so fast that Gomez could hardly catch it. The professor pulled some change from his pocket and gave it to the man, who bowed "thank you" and then looked at Gomez with begging eyes. The man's teeth were rotten and he smelled like mildew and motor oil. Gomez felt in his pocket for his roll of bills. After having saved money for years and having won the Hispanic Scholarship Award from the Grape Growers of America Association, this was the first time that he was able to travel. His father, a postal worker, never had enough money to help him with school, and, in fact, spent most of his life in debt. This beggar must have seen a rich man when he saw Gomez. Although the student was simply dressed in black canvas slacks, a pullover shirt with the Polo emblem at the breast, and comfortable black shoes, each item of clothing, Gomez figured, probably cost more money than the man earned in a year. Still, he wasn't rich, and it seemed a crime to just give money away to this stranger. He felt the roll of bills in his front pocket.

"I don't have any change," he said.

"Anything will be fine," the man said, his eyelids collapsing with sadness and fatigue.

Gomez looked up at Rogstart, who turned away.

"Just go," Gomez said softly.

The man made a show of thanking Rogstart again, looked at Gomez one last time through the thick hair that hung over his face, and then walked off with as much dignity as he could muster.

"Well, Harvey, I hope you have a fine vacation," said the professor.

"Oh, thank you, thank you, sir," Gomez said, as the professor walked off.

At baggage claim, he found the worn, vinyl suitcase that had belonged to his grandparents and dragged it through the airport which seemed to grow bigger and wider with every step, like a coliseum flooded with lights. A boy came up and asked him something, but Gomez didn't understand because he spoke too fast, so the boy asked in English, "Carry your bag, *joven?*"

"Oh, I speak Spanish," Gomez said in English. "I just didn't hear what you said. And no thank you. I'll carry my own bag."

Outside, the heavy, gray air smelled of gasoline and exhaust fumes, and the wide streets were wild with cars and noise. With both hands grasping the handle, he held his suitcase in front of him. Hundreds of taxicabs swarmed around like sharks or were triple parked at the curbs. He looked for a bald red-orange head in the back of the cabs, hoping it wasn't too late to share a ride, but he saw only Mexicans, sometimes entire families squeezed into the back seats. He thought about going back inside the airport to call his father in California and let him know that he had arrived safely, but he wasn't sure how the phone system worked and was too afraid to ask. So he stood, his suitcase getting heavier.

Out the window of his high-rise hotel, he watched the golden angel. She stood on an ivory-colored base in the center of the traffic circle where Avenida de la Reforma meets Insurgentes, her arms raised to the heavens. These were large, wide avenues, the likes of which he had never seen except on postcards or in movies set in Paris. A stream of cars flowed around the circle from all directions, many of them green and white VW Bugs, taxis, which from his window looked like toys. He could see, too, the rooftops of La Zona Rosa, the rich shopping district, and he could see the glass towers of the most expensive hotels sparkling over the dull-colored city. The sun, trying to burst through the blanket of smog, appeared like a vague circle in the gray sky.

He had never been on a plane before, so for the first time he suffered jet lag. Every time he paced the room, it felt as if the floor were moving. He was content to stay in his bed until it passed, like a patient determined to enjoy the rest that sickness brought.

After two days, he rose from his bed, left the room, rode down the elevator, and stepped onto the street. The tunnel of brownstone buildings, crumbling yet dignified, looked like a scene in Europe. Small trees and old street lamps shaped like giant candles rose from the cracked sidewalks. He sighed contentedly. "A beautiful city," he said. Then he went back inside. The next day he was bored enough to leave his room and walk onto the wide, busy avenue toward the golden angel and into the heart of La Zona Rosa. The expensive shops, Gucci, Polo, Yves St. Laurent, relaxed him because they reminded him of Beverly Hills, a place he had once driven through.

He chose an outdoor Italian cafe for lunch and for planning his itinerary, minus the three days he had spent in his room. The weather was sunny and breezy, and the overhanging trees surrounding the buildings kept out the gasoline smell of the city. He was happy.

Then something happened.

The busboy tapped him on the shoulder and said, *"¿Qué 'stas haciendo aquí, primo?"*

In his head, Gomez tried to understand what the guy had said, but he had spoken so fast. "Kay Deesay?" he asked.

The boy looked surprised at Gomez, as if he had expected smooth easy Spanish to flow from his mouth, not slow deliberate words which fell like chunks. "Oh, nothing," the boy said in accented English. "I thought you were . . ." and left on the table a glass of water and a basket of bread.

The waiter took his order in English. As Gomez started eating, he was surprised again when he saw Professor Rogstart, this time coming into the same restaurant. He carried a newspaper under his arm and

sat a few tables away. Gomez was sure the professor would be surprised now. What were the chances of seeing each other twice in the
world's biggest city? Gomez sat silently, hoping the professor would
see him, but he was so preoccupied with his newspaper that he didn't
look up.

Leaning back in his chair, Gomez said, like a movie villain who
has finally trapped the desperate hero, "Well professor, what do you
think now?"

The professor looked up. "Oh, hello, Harvey. How are you
today?" he said, calmly. Gomez took a drink of his water—nervously
hoping it was safe to sip—and said, "Don't tell me that you're not surprised to see me again. This is pretty weird that we see each other, not
once, but twice in the world's biggest city. Wouldn't you say?"

"Actually, I wouldn't," the professor said, patiently folding his
newspaper. "Indeed I find your surprise at this to be the only strange
thing. We're in La Zona Rosa, which is only a four or five block area,
full of people from the U.S. My hotel is here, your hotel is probably
here. It makes complete sense that I would see you, especially at this
restaurant. It's very popular with *gringos*."

Gomez felt like reminding the professor that he wasn't a *gringo*.

"The food is good," the professor continued, "the service is excellent, and the prices reasonable. Completely logical." Then, as if to
further his point, the professor spoke the history of La Zona Rosa, why
it had always been a place for Europeans and Americans to gather.

As Gomez listened, he realized something: Rogstart was enjoying
this conversation, as if they were colleagues talking about some fine
historical point. He wanted to turn the conversation into Spanish so the
waiter and busboys would know what high things they spoke of,
scholars both, but he didn't try because he wasn't sure he could be as
articulate. Still, he listened, nodded his head, and to satisfy that need
to speak Spanish, he said, *"sí, sí"* nodding, nodding, *"Sí,sí,"* with different inflections, and when the professor said something he had
already known, *"Ooooh, síí. sí."* He had always wanted to have a
deep discussion with Rogstart, one of the world's leading historians on
Mexico. He wanted to get up, join him at his table, and they could
spend all day together drinking strong Italian coffee and talking about
history. But after the professor was done lecturing, he looked down at

his newspaper and continued reading. He never invited Gomez to the table. He didn't look up again except for when he left, telling Gomez to have a good day.

When he got his bill, he couldn't believe it was so expensive, a hundred dollars. He wanted to complain but didn't want to seem too cheap. He was going to pay, touching the roll of bills in his front pocket, when he realized, feeling a bit silly, that it was in pesos, not dollars. He left a fifty-peso tip and went back to his hotel room.

The next time the student saw the professor, he suppressed the feeling of surprise. He spotted him at the Aztec ruins which stubbornly stuck from the ground in the downtown plaza, the *zócalo*, between the ancient cathedral and the palace of the government. Rogstart was looking with reverence at a stone slab carved with the faces of Aztec gods. Gomez approached and stood next to him, putting his hands on the rail, and he, too, looked at the faces. One of them had an open mouth and wide eyes as if frightened. Gomez wondered how many Aztecs were scared into believing in their gods, like his father tried to make him believe in Jesus and the Virgin Mary, using stories of Hell and fire, religious baggage he was glad to toss in the closet when he went away to college. Now he was a scholar first and foremost.

As he continued to stare at the masks, he calmly said, "This time I'm not surprised, Professor. You're right, it makes complete sense. You're a scholar of Mexican history, I'm a sch— . . . a student of Mexican history. So it makes a whole lot of sense that we're both here at this Aztec ruin. I mean, doesn't it?"

Rogstart looked at him, surprised. "No, actually, this time I'm surprised."

"Really?"

"I think this qualifies as quite a coincidence," Rogstart said.

"Yeah, I guess so. So, uh, is this the first time you've been here? It is for me."

"I've been here more times than I can count," Rogstart said. "I used to live a few blocks away from here." His eyes suddenly looked dreamy, as if he were about to share some intimate memory with Gomez, but he shook it off and went back to examining the faces. As the silence grew between them, Gomez felt the pressure to say something profound about history, so with a voice that pretended at religious awe, he said, "Think of it: Here was the great city of Tenochtitlan. And the Spaniards destroyed it all. This is all that remains."

Immediately he knew what he had said didn't sound as scholarly as he had hoped, but rather like something a tourist would say. He knew he had to say something else so the words didn't hang in the air like a sign advertising his simplicity.

"How did you get here from La Zona Rosa?" he asked.

"I rode the metro," said the professor.

"Oh. I took a cab."

And it was expensive and the driver, impatient with Gomez' Spanish, wouldn't answer his questions and probably took advantage of him. He suspected that tourists didn't have to pay one hundred pesos more than what the meter read, which was, the cab driver had said, the price for Mexican citizens. He would have asked Professor Rogstart how much he should have paid, but didn't want to appear naive. In fact, as a man with Mexican blood, he should be more knowledgeable than Rogstart, but he had only been to Tijuana one Friday night with a bunch of drunk friends when he was an undergraduate. What he knew about Mexico that was not from a book or from Rogstart was what his grandparents had told him. They had described their tiny ranch in Michoacán, a place he had never seen but often dreamed of, sometimes imagining himself returning to reclaim their land. He pictured the townsfolk, men dressed in white cotton pants and *huaraches,* women in long dresses and flowers in their hair.

The Mexicans are gathered around a gazebo in the town plaza, whispering to each other, wondering who he is, this tall, dark stranger who walks with such authority.

But, of course, he wasn't tall, just dark, very dark.

Now he wanted to take the bus or the metro back to his hotel because it would be cheaper, but he didn't know how and wasn't even sure whom to ask for such directions. It was less intimidating to take a cab, but expensive. He hadn't that much money. He put his hand in his pant pocket to feel the roll. It was still there, but thinner than before.

He watched as Rogstart stared at the masks.

He asked the professor, "When are you going back?"

"To California?" the professor asked.

"No, to La Zona Rosa," Gomez said.

"Later."

Gomez said, "Do you mind if I tag along with you? I mean, maybe you can show me some things."

Rogstart didn't say anything. He sighed discontentedly, and, as if he hadn't heard him, he said, "I'm off, Harvey. Have a good day."

"Can I come with you? I mean, for a little while?"

Rogstart put his hands on his hips and looked around the sky. "Sure. I guess. Come on."

For the first time Gomez was able to enjoy Mexico City. They went to the palace of the government and saw the Diego Rivera murals that depicted the Spanish conquest of Mexico. Rogstart, feeling a professorial obligation, explained to Gomez the meaning of each panel, each symbol, giving such fine details that other tourists stopped and listened, too; and some, as if students in his class, asked questions. Gomez felt a sense of pride as Rogstart spoke and the people listened, like a boy proud of his father. When one of the tourists asked a question about an historical fact, Rogstart turned to Gomez and said, "I think Professor Gomez can answer that one."

Gomez was high. "Yes, I uh, think the best way to answer that is to consider the lifestyle of the *mayaque*, which was, essentially, the Aztec *peon* . . ."

People listened.

On the way out, as they descended the wide stairs to the bottom floor, Rogstart pulled from his pant pocket a box of mints, shook a few of the green pellets into his palm, threw them in his mouth, and sucked, his jaw moving back and forth. Then he held the tiny box to Gomez, who gladly opened his palm.

They walked through the *zócalo*. He wanted to invite Rogstart to a nice place for lunch. He felt in his pocket for the roll of bills, wondering where Rogstart would choose and how much it would cost.

They walked past the booths where Indians and mestizos sold T-shirts, jewelry, and handmade dolls dressed like the New Zapatistas in Chiapas. The professor stopped at a booth where an Indian woman sold what looked to Gomez like thick blue tortillas smothered with some sort of grey-green paste. It looked sickening to him, but the professor was apparently excited as he waited for the lady to prepare his. He turned around and asked Gomez if he wanted one, too. "No, no, thank you," he said. "In fact, I was going take you to lunch, sir. If you want."

"This is enough for me," Rogstart said, turning around to watch the lady prepare his food.

Gomez noticed a booth where someone was selling used books. He walked over and looked at the titles and saw an old copy of *México Viejo*, a history book. The vendor, a young man with long hair and beard, watched. When he asked how much he wanted for the book, the vendor looked him up and down, as if it were Gomez that was being sold. "Fifty pesos," he said.

Gomez, wondering if it was worth it, turned to ask Rogstart.

The professor was happily eating his fat blue tortilla. Gomez stepped toward him, but between them came a stream of Aztec dancers, young people with plumed head dresses. One of the dancers waved and said something to the young bookseller.

When the stream of dancers passed, Rogstart wasn't in the same spot.

Gomez walked over to the food booth and looked around, but he couldn't see the familiar head in the crowd.

Then the *zócalo* exploded with voices, car horns, and thumping of feet of thousands of people. The Aztec dancers began their dance by blowing a horn and ritually facing the four directions, the leader holding a vase of burning sage to the heavens. They wore colorful, feathered costumes and had bare feet, with ankle bracelets of clanking nuts. The twirling of feathers and bodies made the sound of wind through trees.

He turned toward the lady selling the food, who held out a plate and asked if he wanted one. Unconsciously, he held his stomach, as if he might vomit, and said, in broken Spanish, no thank you, but did she see what happened to the tall white guy who was standing here eating? The lady laughed, her broken teeth showing through the flabby, wrinkled mouth.

He turned around, and a man and a woman stood in front of him, their palms open, faces twisted with hunger. They said, *Un peso por favor*.

"Get away from me," he said.

He spun around and walked through the *zócalo* searching for his professor. Other beggars, ladies, children, old men were determined to get something from him, anything. They practically surrounded him. *Un peso por favor.*

"No!" he screamed, breaking through and running deeper into the plaza, looking for that red-orange bald head. The young man at the book booth yelled, *"¿Y Mexico Viejo? ¿No quieres México Viejo?"*

He went into the cathedral hoping the professor might be there, because it was the first cathedral in Mexico and of great historical significance.

Inside he felt a spirit of peace in the air, but every time it tried to enter him, he resisted and went on walking deeper into the darkness, the ancient walls rising around him like canyons of a desert. All the voices of the tourists and worshipers were as one, the sound of wind whispering off walls. The interior was held up by crisscrossing metal scaffolds. The further he went into the belly of the cathedral, the darker it got and the more things glowed: statues of saints, Jesus, and La Virgen, gold crosses, communion goblets.

He sat at a wooden pew before one of the altars and caught his breath. He knew Rogstart would be in here, and this time, when he saw him, he wouldn't let him go. He would beg, plead if he had to, *please, let me follow you around*, for the rest of the trip, not as his equal, but as a student, a servant if Rogstart wanted. He'd even carry his luggage. The city scared him.

But Rogstart was nowhere in the cathedral.

Gomez ran, still determined to find him, into sunlight and smog. At the cathedral gate, a lady with one foot, her wound white with pus and slimy red, her eyes brimming with pain, sat holding up an empty hand. She said to Gomez, looking into his eyes, *por favor, por favor*, but he ran around her, through the *zócalo*. He remembered that the museum of Bellas Artes was nearby, so he asked what looked like a white tourist for directions. He ran out of the *zócalo*, through a narrow downtown street whose tall, old buildings rose up around him like the walls of a dark, cold dungeon. He passed little ladies sitting on blankets selling *chicle*, skinny children with their open palms raised, lone men sitting on curbs, mangy dogs sniffing for food. He ran all the way to the museum, a grand structure shining like a white mosque in the middle of the gray city. He paid the twenty pesos to get in and looked around, not at art, but for Rogstart.

He never found him, and an hour later he sat on the wide steps of the museum.

He didn't care how much it would cost. He didn't care that the driver might make fun of his Spanish or roll his eyes when he spoke English; he didn't care that he had come so far from home and had not seen or would not see anything he had come to see, Chapúltepec Park, the Museum of Anthropology, the pyramids. All he cared about was getting a taxi back to his hotel, where he would close the curtains in his room and lay on the bed—for the rest of the vacation. He hated Mexico. He'd order room service and watch TV. Might even change his graduate school emphasis to European History.

Across the street, several taxis were lined up at the curb, so he stood up and walked toward them. He slipped his hand into his pocket for his roll of bills. When he didn't feel the money there, he felt, for a flash, a sense of panic, but he chuckled at his foolishness when he figured he had put it in his other pocket.

He put his hand in the other pocket.

Empty.

"Oh shit," he said as he patted his back pockets. "Oh, shit, no."

His shirt pockets.

"Oh, God no," he whispered. "Please, God, don't do this to me." He felt his ankles just in case he forgot that he had put it in his socks, but all he felt was bone.

"Oh shit. Oh shit. Oh shit," he chanted as he walked around in circles, trying not to panic, trying to believe there was some explanation.

But all that came to him was that he had lost it.

"No. No."

He walked quickly up the wide stairs of the museum, but a security guard pulled him by the arm and told him something in Spanish.

"I paid already," Gomez said, but the man, wearing a blue suit and tie with a wire to his ear like a Secret Service agent, calmly shrugged his shoulders to show he didn't understand English. He pointed to the ticket window downstairs.

"Please," said Gomez, about to cry, as if saying it made it more true: "I just lost all my money. Please, I have to look!"

The guard began to lead Gomez down the stairs, but the student twisted from his grip and ran up. "Sorry," he yelled. "I have to find it."

It was all he had, the whole roll. And because he had feared that the hotel maid would go through his things and find it, he hadn't left any of it in his room. He ran, chanting, "Oh, no, oh no, no no no no."

People stepped out of the way and watched him and the two security guards chasing him. He ran up another flight of stairs. And then he saw it. On the ground, the cash wad reflecting on the shiny floor. "Oh, thank you," he whispered as he shifted into a higher gear, running as fast as he could. Before he got to it, he slid to a stop as if he were on ice. He bent down and grabbed a crumpled up, empty pack of cigarettes. The security guards grabbed him by both arms.

"I lost my money," he cried, as they dragged him outdoors, all the way across the museum plaza, and discarded him on the sidewalk.

He ran back to the *zócalo*, searched the floors of the cathedral, the government palace, and then found, standing side by side watching the dancers, the young book vendor and the lady with the blue tortillas. He asked them if they had seen a roll of money, at which they looked at each other and laughed.

After he didn't know where to look anymore, he walked back and forth from the museum to the *zócalo,* his arms out, as if grabbing for something in the air, a gesture of which he wasn't conscious. Dirt and dust had gotten on his clothes and his hair was disheveled. He had no credit cards, no ATM card. He couldn't call his father, who had no money and would just call him an idiot. If he didn't find Rogstart, then he had no hope. He mumbled *No no no no no.*

A white couple, walking hand and hand in his direction, saw him and averted their gaze. One young American girl, a hippie in her twenties, dressed in a peasant skirt and with her hair in braids, watched him with compassionate blue eyes, and when he passed, she said, *"¿Señor?"* and put a coin in his extended hand. He kept walking, without panic because shock had set in. At an outdoor cafe, he approached a blue-eyed man eating his lunch. "I lost all my money. All my money."

The man wore an expensive suit and tie. He shrugged his shoulders and said, *"No hablo inglés,"* and gave Gomez some coins. Gomez turned around and, without looking to see if it were safe, crossed a narrow side street. A taxi braked to avoid hitting him and the driver honked the horn, angrily raising his fist in the air, but when Gomez—with a wave of his hand—indicated that he needed a cab, the driver smiled and nodded and pulled over.

"I don't speak Spanish," he said, as he entered. "Take me to the Zona Rosa."

"I thought you were Mexican," said the cab driver.

"No, no I'm not. The Zona Rosa please."

"Yes, sir," the driver said. He was a chubby-faced man with large, gold eyes and a balding head.

The cab pulled onto the street. A picture dangled from the rear view mirror, the sacred, bloody heart of Jesus. Gomez leaned back, and for some reason he felt relaxed. He knew that he would have to find a way to run from the cab before it got to his hotel, but he would bother with the details later, because it was a long drive.

He hoped.

"I don't have a meter," said the driver, looking over his shoulder at Gomez.

"That's okay."

"It cost one hundred pesos."

"That's fine," said Gomez. And it felt good saying it. Charge me two hundred, he might have told the driver.

"You are visiting Mexico for pleasure?"

"Pure pleasure," Gomez said, and that made him feel even better, more relaxed.

"Have you go to the Basílica? *Muy* beautiful."

"No, not yet."

"I take you there. I can show you many beautiful places."

Gomez nodded, acknowledging his offer. At an intersection they waited at a red light, where a dark, dirty young man stood facing the line of waiting cars, as if he were on stage and they were the audience. With a flourish he held up a flaming stick in one hand and an old plastic milk container in the other. He drank from the container and put the flame into his mouth and blew out fire like a dragon. He did this several times and then bowed for applause. He went to the car windows with an open hand. Most people ignored him through their closed windows, but a few gave. When he got to Gomez, he said, *"Por favor."* Gomez handed him the coins the people had given him. The cab driver, watching through the rear view mirror, smiled.

When they got close to La Zona Rosa, Gomez began to worry. How could he escape? The cab was a VW Bug and he would have to flee from the passenger's side, somehow lifting the front seat, grabbing the door handle and jumping out. He looked down the side streets to see where he might run.

That's when he saw him walking into a fancy hotel made of glass: Professor David P. Rogstart.

Then the cab pulled over. "Here we are," said the driver.

He was going to yell out the window, "Professor, Help!" but something stopped him, some nagging deep in his heart. He looked in the rear view mirror at the cab driver's gaze, those large eyes, and he thought of his father. When Gomez had told him about the trip, his father, who hardly ever had something good to say, was actually proud. Gomez could tell.

"I never been there," he told his son, unbuttoning his postal worker's jacket.

"It's the biggest city in the world," Gomez said.

"Yeah, that's good," said the father. "Maybe you're not such a big dummy after all."

"I changed my mind," Gomez said to the cab driver.

"What is that?" asked the driver.

"I don't want the Zona Rosa."

"No?"

He looked out the window. "Take me to Chapúltepec Park."

"Oh, yes," said the driver, seeming very happy. "It's beautiful there. You must see the castle where jumped *los niños herores*. You know this story?" he asked.

"Yeah, yeah, take me there. And after that let's go to Garibaldi Square."

"You like the music of mariachis, eh?"

"I love it," said Gomez. "Love it."

"*Ay,* see?" said the driver, pointing his finger at Gomez, "You *are* a Mexican!"

They laughed as the taxi pulled into traffic.

Ofrenda

When I was two months old, my dead mother held me in her arms. My brother Vern showed me the black and white photo. In front of golden drapes that reached the ground, she held me with one arm and with the other hand free, she touched my nose. The lamp in the room made me bright, a little bundle wrapped in white, glowing on her hand and face. "Wow. That's mom?" I said.

I was fourteen and had never seen her before, because she died two months after the photo was taken. She looked nothing like I had pictured. She was sexy and tall, wearing tight nylon pants and a snug blouse.

"She's pretty beautiful, isn't she?" Vern said, sitting shirtless on his bed. He was nineteen, but even with the room lights dim, he looked to be in his thirties, splotchy beard, bony arms and chest. In less than a year he would die of AIDS.

"I want you to have it," he said.

"Thanks," I said. I took it back to the house and when I went to bed I held it on my chest. After I was sure Mr. and Mrs. Martin were asleep, I flicked on the light and looked at it again. Under the brightness, I could see her much clearer. She had light brown hair and a face shaped like a heart. Then I noticed she wasn't wearing a bra, her breasts shaped like . . . simply like the sloping breasts of a beautiful woman. I ran my finger up and down her image. "Hi, mom," I said, "I'm your son."

At school, I showed the photo to my best friend Raul Galivan. "I'd do her any day," he said.

"That's my mother, you idiot," I said.

"No shit?" He grabbed the photo and looked closer. "I think I see her nipples," he said.

Jimmy Strunk, an eleventh grader, who didn't have a mother or father, walked by and looked over my shoulder. He had a scar that ran from his chin to his neck, and red hair and freckles. He said, looking at the photo, "Damn. That lady's so fine I'd eat the corn out of her shit."

"That's sick," I said. "That's my mother."

"So what are you going to do about it?" he said. Shortly after he would turn eighteen, he would go to prison for murder.

"I'm just saying it's my mother," I said.

One day Mrs. Reinholt, the Spanish teacher, told us about the Day of the Dead. We would erect altars, she said, called *ofrendas*, and we would display them in the cafeteria as a class project. "Bring a photo of someone who died, that you were close to," she said. On tables, around the photos, we would place things that the deceased liked while they were still among us. Things they liked to eat or drink.

I would use her picture for the altar, I decided. I called Vern at the hospital to ask what things mom liked. He was five when she died so he didn't remember much. "Wait a minute," he said. He coughed away from the phone. Then he said, out of breath, "I think she liked grape-fruit."

"What about dad, would he know?" I asked.

"Do you really want to call dad?" he asked.

Even if he were sober enough to recognize my name and voice, he would think I wanted money. He would live a long time, an old, unhappy man.

"No, I guess not," I said.

I tried to picture mom opening presents under a Christmas tree, but couldn't picture what she would want to pull from the boxes. I decided, maybe she did like grapefruit, so that's what I put around her photo. I also placed bowls of candy, loaves of bread, and *calaveras*, sugar skulls. The Spanish class had about twenty tables in the cafeteria.

For two days I spent the entire lunch period before the *ofrendas*. The one time Raul Galivan talked me into going outside to watch some girls play volleyball, I felt my mother calling me to come back, so I left him in the sun and returned to the cafeteria. Before her altar, I felt peace, like resting in shadow. Except when Jimmy Strunk walked by. He would bend over her table and look at the photo, and then he made a masturbation gesture with his fist.

One day I went in the cafeteria and her picture was missing.

"Well, shit, what do you expect?" said Raul. "With that nipple and all."

I stood in the crowded cafeteria and yelled, "Whoever took that photo, I'm going to kick your ass!"

Raul tried to talk sense into me. "Did you forget you don't know how to fight?"

Some of the varsity football players who sat together laughed. Then some of the *cholos* hanging out on the other side of the cafeteria laughed at me too. One yelled, "Oh, we're so scared."

But I was beside myself. "I'm not kidding. I'll make this my fucking crusade. I want that picture back."

Then I saw him sitting alone, like he always did, in the corner of the cafeteria, laughing and watching as he ate a sandwich. Jimmy Strunk, his curly red hair disheveled and high on his head like an afro. I pointed at him, "I'll kick your ass, Jimmy."

He stood and walked over to me, slowly. I could hear from around the cafeteria, "Boy's going to get his ass kicked." "He's dead." Even the jocks and *cholos* didn't mess with Jimmy Strunk, yet here I was, the smallest kid in school.

Jimmy stood right in front of me. "What you going to do, huh?"

"Did you take my mother's picture?" I said, cried really, my voice cracking.

He looked around, and everyone was watching. The scar running down his chin was purple. "What if I did?" he said, looking in my eyes.

"I'll kill you," I said, looking in his.

"Oooh!" said the students.

"Do it," he said, coming in closer. "Do it." He was so close I could smell the tuna on his breath. "Do it," he breathed.

Suddenly I pictured the photo. My mother cooed at me and smiled, her eyes wide with awe, as if she held a miracle. Then she looked up at the camera, right at the lens. "Do it," she said. "Do it."

So warm. Like shadow.

"Here," said Jimmy, pulling the photo from his back pocket and handing it to me. "It was just a fucking joke." He walked back to his seat and sat alone. Everyone watched me, some came up to me and patted my back and talked to me. But I kept watching him, alone in the corner, where he finished chewing his bitter sandwich.

Expression of Our People

This huge white guy walked into the cafeteria, followed by a cloud of dust and feathers. This guy was enormous, fat and tall, shoulders as wide as a VW Bug. He walked fast, as if he was going to a fight that he knew he would win. Then he just stopped and looked around. It was seven, lunchtime for the swing shift, so the place was full and everybody seemed to be watching him, probably hoping he wouldn't sit next to them. He had long dirty blonde hair in a ponytail, and his plump face, scrunched up, scrutinizing, made it seem as if he were looking for an enemy. He caught me looking at him and walked over to my table, where I sat alone. He sat right across from me, bringing this nasty stench with him. From a brown paper bag he pulled out three sandwiches wrapped in waxed paper, a fat chunk of homemade cake with yellow frosting, and two cans of soda.

I was eating one of those frozen burritos you buy from the machines, "green burrito" it said on the wrapping, but it wasn't green and the tortilla tasted like typing paper.

He looked like one of those big white guys who rides a Harley Davidson, and he had a tattoo on his neck, "ESF," and I had no idea what it meant. He had other tattoos, little green crosses, between his thumbs and fingers. We didn't say anything, we just ate, and when the buzzer went off, we got up and went our separate ways.

After that day, every time this big fuck slammed into the building, he looked around for me and sat by me. I wasn't hard to spot, because everyone at the plant was either Mexican or Sikh, real Indians, with turbans and the whole bit, and they spoke in their own languages. My hair was long, almost to my butt, which during lunch I took out of the hair net and let fall free. So he sat by me and started eating. After a while, I got used to the smell. One day, as he was chewing a fat home-made burrito—and for this guy one bite was half the burrito—he looked at me, his brows furled, like he was suspicious of me. "You an Indian?' he said.

"Apache," I said.

"Peacock," he said.

"What the fuck is that?" I said.

"My name, asshole," he said.

A few days later, I was eating one of those egg salad sandwiches from the machine, the kind that are cut in two triangles and taste too sweet, like they sprinkled sugar on it. The bread was soggy, so I was a little irritated to begin with when Peacock, spooning chili from a Tupperware bowl into his mouth and chewing on a fat slab of meat, said, "I'm Navajo."

"That's pretty damn interesting," I said.

He slammed his hand on the table. "What the hell do you mean by that?" he said. His eyes looked threateningly into mine.

I hadn't been living in Fresno for too long, which as far as I could tell was one big city of poverty and violence, but I knew what it meant to guys like him if I lowered my head or averted my gaze, so I stared into his eyes. "What I mean, white boy," I said, "is I don't care how Indian you think you are."

He stood up, slapped his wide palms on the tabletop and bent over toward me. "Fuck you!" he yelled, loud enough so everyone looked over at us, probably hoping to see me slaughtered.

"My dad was full blood," he said. "Lived on the rez."

"Sit down, whitey," I said.

He plopped in his seat, dust rising up around him, and he pointed a fat finger at me. He wore a wedding ring, a tight gold band. "You know what you are?" he said, looking at the name tag sewed onto my work overalls. "Sanchez," he said, in two syllables, as if the name revealed some shameful secret about me. "You know what you are, Sanchez? Redder than thou. You're fucking redder than thou."

I didn't bother telling him that the name tag was already sewed on the uniform when I started working for the plant and that my last name was Carter. Freddy Carter.

My job was cutting the multi-colored entrails from dead chickens that came by hanging upside down on shackles. I was from Arizona, but I had moved to Fresno to live with my brother, who had gone to school here and who worked for a non-profit job-training program for the poor. His wife had a better job, at least she made more than he did, so they invited me to come, and since I wasn't doing anything on the rez but watching my life go by, reflected on the backs of cockroaches, I took them up on the offer. The first few weeks they tried to talk me into going to the community college, because I was smart, they said, but I wasn't interested. I read newspapers and watched TV for a couple of months, and at night I stared at my ceiling or went out in the backyard to hang out with the dogs, who were always fighting each other unless I was there between them, petting them equally on their dumb-looking heads. Then one night my brother came into the little windowless room where I lived, sat on my cot and told me I needed to start working. He was a job counselor, so I could be working the next day. He held before me a deck of cards, each one printed with a low-paying, non-skilled job. I think he figured hard work would make me want to go to school. "Take your pick," he said, fanning out the cards like a Las Vegas dealer.

"What's that one?" I said, pointing randomly.

He read it. "Chicken plant," he said. "You want to kill chickens, Freddy?"

"Sign me up," I said.

As the lady from the personnel office showed me my locker, she started talking to me in Spanish. "I ain't Mexican," I said.

"Okay," she said, throwing me the overalls. "I believe you."

One day Peacock came into the cafeteria without lunch from home. He stood across from me and fished in his pockets for some coins, which he counted to himself, his lips moving like he had to concentrate real hard. "What you eating there?" he said.

It was a frozen pizza turnover, which tasted like shit, because the sauce was sour, like rotten liver paste. "Haute cuisine," I said.

"How much?"

"A dollar fifty."

He counted, then looked around at the machines and went to get one.

The following day, payday, he followed me to the car. I didn't see him, but I felt his presence, like a shadow behind my back. He walked up to the passenger door.

"What?" I said.

"Let's go get a beer," he said.

I got in and unlocked the passenger's door. He brought the smell with him. As we drove through the city, we didn't talk, but just let the streetlights and neon blur by us. It was about midnight and things were crazy, kids driving around in their cars, prostitutes hanging around the phone booths of 7-11, fourteen-year-old gangbangers walking like men along the dark sidewalks.

"This your car?" he said.

"My brother's," I said.

"Looks like a rez car," he said, meaning it was all beat up.

Peacock tuned radio stations in and out until he found a song he liked, a country western tune. He snapped his fingers. "This music gets me in touch with my white side," he said.

We passed a little bar in a wooden building, The Silver Spike. In front was a lit up sign on trailer wheels that said "Live Country Music" and "Drink Specials."

"Let's go there," he said. "Hang out with the cowboys."

I pulled into the gravel lot. "Are you sure about this?" I said.

"You scared, Pancho?"

"Not of them," I said. "Of myself. You've never seen me drunk," I said.

"Let's go party," he said.

"Seriously, man, you don't know what I'm like." I could have told him stories. I could have shown him scars. "And I ain't drank in a long time. Things could get weird. Especially in a place like this with all the rednecks."

"Don't worry," he said. "I got your back."

We got out and walked through the gravel, the sound of tiny bones crunching beneath our feet. At the wooden door, beyond which we could hear muffled music, we looked at each other. Peacock nodded. I nodded back. He pulled open the door.

Of course, Peacock was a big fuck, so although some of the cowboys looked at us like they was wondering what the hell we were doing there, they looked away when he stared at them. One tall cowboy in a white hat and with a moustache didn't look away. He looked like the Marlboro Man, standing by the bar, his thumbs in the waist of his belt, fingers pointing toward the bulge in his tight jeans. He wore a leather western vest and a cowboy shirt. He looked at us, his eyes squinted, and he looked around at other people, too, as if wondering if there would be trouble. I figured he was the manager or the owner because he kept telling people who worked there what to do. After a while, he quit watching us. It was a good thing Peacock didn't see him, because there might have been trouble, although the drunker I got the more the Marlboro Man irritated me. He walked around the place like he was at a dude ranch and we were his cattle. I felt like smashing his nose.

But what I saw next made me forget that I wanted to fight. Or who I saw next.

She was serving cocktails.

"Damn," I said.

She was clearly a native, long black hair, black eyes, her facial features sharp and strong. She was wearing real tight jeans and a T-shirt a few sizes too small. "Damn," I said. I turned to Peacock. "You like Indian girls?" I said.

"I got me a girl," he said. And then he looked at his beer bottle, as if it were whispering something to him.

The girl was at the bar now, where the waitresses order their drinks, her back toward us. I mean, she looked damn good from behind, kind of like if you just walked into the place and that was all you saw of her, you'd know that on the other side of her, she would be just as good, because if not, something's wrong with the world. I was drunk.

"I'll be back," I said to Peacock, who didn't seem to hear me but was still looking at his bottle.

So I walked up behind her and stood right next to her, her profile so close, and her face so beautiful, so native. She was waiting for the bartender, some skinny nerdy guy with a cowboy hat, so she could give him her order. "Hey," I said, "what tribe are you?"

This seemed to surprise her. She looked me up and down and said, "You made me forget my order." She seemed like she was trying to appear pissed, but I think she was flirting. "Now let's see," she said, still looking at me, counting on her fingers, "three Buds, two Lights, a bourbon seven, a screwdriver . . ."

"Well, I've been living in this town for four months and I ain't seen many other skins until tonight, until you."

"I'm trying to remember my order," she said.

"Freddy," I said.

"Freddy," she said, like she was chastising a child, "Emily's trying to remember her order."

I figured she slipped in her name on purpose.

The bartender came, leaned over toward her, and she told him her order. As he made them, she relaxed and looked over at me. "What are you?" she said.

"Apache," I said.

"I'm Sioux," she said.

I laughed.

"What's so funny?"

"You're lying, Emily," I said. "You ain't no Sioux."

And then I walked back to the table, where Peacock had a shot of tequila waiting for me. "Fuck it," he said, as I sat. "Let's get drunk," he said.

"*Get* drunk?" I said.

I didn't even look at Emily the rest of the night and even danced with a couple of cowgirls. One of them, a voluptuous girl in tight jeans and with a bunch of blonde hair that smelled like cigarette smoke and that was stiff with hairspray, kept running her sweaty fingers through my hair, saying how beautiful it was. From certain angles she wasn't all that bad-looking, but when she invited me to sit with her, I said no thanks and went back to the table where Peacock was so drunk he swayed from side to side as he sat in his chair.

Then Emily came to our table, her arms crossed like she was mad at me. "What do you mean I'm a liar?" she said. "How dare you!"

"You ain't no Sioux," I said.

"Are not," she corrected.

"What kind of Sioux are you?" I said.

"What kind?" she said. "What kind of question is that? I'm Sioux, a Sioux Sioux."

"From where?" I said.

"Uh, Oregon," she said.

"You don't know shit about the Sioux," I said.

She put her hands on her hips (she was fucking beautiful). "And you do I suppose."

"I know all kinds of things," I said.

"Like what?"

Then the band announced last call and said they'd do one more song. "I ain't got time to tell you all the things I know," I said. "Better give me your phone number."

"Ha! You think I give out my number that easy?" Then her boss, Marlboro Man, tapped her on the shoulder. He put his hand on her waist and pulled her a bit closer, and with the rim of his white cowboy hat, he pointed toward her tables, meaning get back to work. After she left, he stood there and looked at me, his thumbs still in his belt, and I was about to tell him to get the fuck out of my face, before he walked away. I felt like punching him, just because he was so arrogant and it would probably make me feel real good. On our way out of the club, Peacock was singing out loud and slapping cowboys on the back, saying "What's up, pardner?" Emily came up behind me and slipped a piece of paper in my palm.

"If you turn out to be a psycho," she said, "I swear I'll never forgive you."

I was still drunk when I got home—even after I went to Fat Burger with Peacock and almost got in a fight with some black guys until some cops pulled into the parking lot. I didn't even think about it when I picked up the phone and dialed Emily's number. It was 4 a.m.

"I knew it," she said, "you're a psycho."

We talked for hours, as I walked around the kitchen, until the sun rose over the fence and lit up the dirt floor of my brother's backyard. I could see the dogs, of different breeds, sleeping on opposite sides.

She told me she didn't know anything about her tribe because her adopted parents were white, so she never got to know anything about her true family.

"Who knows," she said, "You could be my brother."

"Don't say that," I said, "that's sick."

"Why's that sick?" she said.

As I was cutting guts off the chickens, Peacock slammed into the work area. He was a live-hanger, one of the workers that pulled the reluctant chickens from the cages when they were still alive and fighting, and that was a real dirty job, so he wasn't allowed in our part of the plant. Everyone was watching him walk toward me. The foreman saw him and he started asking Peacock what the hell's going on here, but Peacock didn't stop. He was coming right at me. By the time he reached me there were three foremen behind him, all of them looking nervous, hoping this big guy wasn't going to go crazy and start killing people.

"What happened?" he said. "I don't remember a thing about last night."

"We ended up at Fat Burger," I said. "You slept in the car most of the time."

I looked at the foremen and they were looking at me like they were pleading with me to get this giant out of here.

"Peacock," I said. "Why don't you go back to work. We'll talk at lunch."

He turned around. He looked at the foremen. They looked scared.

Peacock suddenly screamed, *Ahhhhhhh!,* so close to them and so loudly that they closed their eyes and scrunched up their faces as if they were in a sandstorm. Then he laughed at them. Then he winked at me and left.

"What's wrong with him?" one of the foremen asked me.

"He's a crazy," another one said.

"He's freaking out," I said. "He needs to be around his people."

"What you mean? White people?"

"No, me."

"You're not white," the foreman said.

"Neither is he," I said.

At lunchtime Peacock hung out by the vending machines until he found things he wanted, and then he came back with an armful of packaged food, which he dumped on the table. He sat down, unwrapped the first thing, and gobbled it up.

"What happened?" I said. "How come you haven't been bringing your own lunch?"

He shook his head, as if the subject was off-limits.

Suddenly, this Mexican, thinking I was Mexican, came up to me and started speaking Spanish, but I didn't know what the hell he was saying. I was about to tell him he was wasting his time, but Peacock surprised the shit out of me. He started talking in Spanish, fast too, like he had been speaking it all his life, pointing to something by the door, explaining something to the Mexican, who kept nodding his head saying, *"Claro, claro."*

When the guy, left, Peacock opened another package of food and started eating again.

"Where the hell did you learn that?" I said.

He shrugged his shoulders and ate.

I looked at the tattoo on is neck. "What does that mean?" I said. "ESF."

"Something from my past," he said.

"A gang?" I said.

"What is this, an interview?"

"Ok, what do you want to talk about?"

"Last night. Did we get in a fight?"

"No," I said.

"Let's go back tonight," he said. "Maybe we'll have better luck."

I had thought by the end of our phone conversation, that Emily was interested in me.

"Come on in tomorrow night and I'll buy you a drink," she had said.

"A drink?" I said.

Maybe I was feeling the effects of the booze, but it bothered me to see her flirt with other tables of guys, just like she was flirting with me and Peacock, and I wondered if she begged them to come to the bar too. This was probably her way of making good money, like she said she made. Peacock was too drunk to know what was going on. Every time she came to the table, he tipped her a dollar.

"We need another shot," Peacock now said. "Where's Emily?" he said. She was across the bar, bending down over some table where two cowboys were sitting drinking long necks and looking down her blouse probably. Peacock stood up and yelled like a cowboy. He was louder than the band and they looked kind of pissed that he would take their attention away.

"Emily!" he screamed. She and the cowboys looked at Peacock, and she gave him a mean cold look.

So she walked toward us like she was about ready to scold us. She was wearing real tight shorts, her leg muscles flexing, tense, hard, with each step. When she reached our table, she looked at me—not Peacock—like I messed up real bad or something.

"Freddy," she said, "I got to talk to you."

"What?" I said.

"In private. I'll meet you in the back room."

"Another round," Peacock blurted out, like he was throwing up or something.

"I'll get you some coffee," she said.

"Fuck that," he said. "I want some booze, baby."

He was half-conscious.

"Emily'll bring some coffee," I said.

I saw her going through the curtains to the back room, so I followed her and went in there too. We were in one of those extra rooms that they opened up if it got real busy. It was dark inside, and she was sitting at a little bar table, her legs crossed. I sat down. I thought she was going to scold me about Peacock, but she said, "I want to go out with you. But I want to pay for everything. Would you feel threatened by that?"

"Hell no," I said.

"Well, I just wanted to make sure."

"Fine with me."

"I really liked talking with you the other night, Freddy."

"Me too," I said.

This moment was so nice and tender, but I was so drunk, so of course I had to say something stupid. "Are we going to sleep together?" I said.

"What the hell's that got to do with it?" she asked.

"I really want to sleep with you," I said.

"Remember what I said," she said. "No psychos."

Just then a tall man with a cowboy hat filled the entrance, blocking the light coming in from the bar. The Marlboro Man. "Don't you have tables?" he asked. His voice was deep and slow.

"Sure, boss," Emily said. She told me we'd talk later, and then she walked up to the boss, but he didn't get out of her way so she could pass. He looked at me. "Your friend looks like he had a few too many," he said.

"Maybe we'll have a few more," I said.

He grinned, slowly nodded his head, then he looked at Emily. "No more for the big guy," he told her. Then he turned around and walked out. Emily followed him, without looking at me.

I waited for the Marlboro Man in the parking lot. The place emptied out, people stood by their cars for a while, and some couples made out. "You going to kick his ass?" asked Peacock.

"Either that or I'm going to dance with him," I said. "I ain't decided yet."

I was drunk enough and unreasonable enough that I would have messed with him, hadn't Emily walked out of the bar and seen me. She walked over to my window, and thinking that I was waiting for her, she said, "You guys want to go get some coffee?"

One weekend we drove to the coast, to Carmel, in Emily's Tercel. It was dark by the time we got there and we didn't much enjoy walking around and looking in the little shops and walking past the restaurants and coffee houses because there was just a bunch of rich people hanging around spending money. We looked through the window of a Native American shop. We saw blankets and jewelry and traditional headgear, things that native people made, costing a thousand times more than what it cost to make.

"How do you feel about that?" Emily asked.

"Well, I don't mind that it's so expensive. These people can afford it. What bothers me is the way the owners of these places exploit the native crafts people."

"You're pretty smart," she said. "I mean, I wouldn't have gone out with you, Freddy, if you were just handsome."

"You think I'm handsome?"

"Oh, stop it," she said. "You should go to school. You can start at Fresno City College."

"Why would I go to school? It's just white shit anyway."

"Oh, come on, you're too smart to believe that. I'm doing all right in social work. I'm learning a lot about how to help people. It's important."

"Our people don't need social workers. We need guns."

"What?"

"No, I don't mean that. It's just the universities are the training grounds for white leaders. It's a waste of time. I don't want to train to be white."

"Well, I think you could get what you want from it," she said. "I've taken Native American Studies classes that were pretty straight forward from a native perspective."

"If you want a native perspective, go to the rez," I said. "Hey, look," I said, pointing between two buildings. Two walruses, wet and black, were sitting on the rocks, their coats reflecting light and water, waves slapping against the rocks. "Let's go check it out."

We sat for a while listening to the ocean, and then she said. "I think you're right—to an extent—about school. It's very white, all these theories and histories. But you know something? You're all I have that's not white. Funny, huh? And I'm full-blooded . . . something . . . some tribe. I mean, I must be full-blooded: look at me."

We spent the night in a motel in Salinas. We took a walk to Taco Bell late that night where a bunch of white teenagers were hanging out by their pickups, and we drank iced tea in silence.

When we got back to the motel, we went to bed, and Emily told me she sure wished I would do something with my life other than kill chickens. "You'd make a good lawyer," she said. "You can be very persuasive."

"I like killing chickens," I said. She put her arms around me, breathed warm breath into my ear. "I like you, Freddy."

Monday a foreman pulled me off the line and said I was needed outside because Peacock was going crazy.

"He's tearing the heads off the fucking chickens," he said.

By the time I got to the brick room where the live-hangers worked, Peacock was sitting on a pile of dead chickens, blood all over himself. If the hangers pulled a dead chicken off the truck, they would throw it into a pile in the corner. That's where Peacock was sitting. He didn't kill all those chickens himself.

"Hey," he said when he saw me. "Grab a chicken, sit down."

I sat next to him. We sat for a while without words.

Then I said, "What's up?"

"She went back to Mexico," he said. "She hates everything about this country."

"Why don't you go with her?" I said.

"Wasn't invited," he said.

The foreman peeked his skinny head from behind the door and Peacock, seeing him, grabbed a headless chicken and hurled at him. The foremen's mouth opened wide, and he disappeared.

"You better quit this shit," I said after a few minutes.

"How come?"

"White people can't handle it when we express ourselves."

She had lived all her life in LA. with her adopted parents, but as soon as she could manage it, when she was eighteen, she packed the '74 Datsun B210 she had bought by working after school, and she drove out of the city and just kept driving north, through the mountains, gliding down into the yellow sea of the valley, and then flat driving for hundreds of miles past fields and farms until she got to Fresno, one hundred square miles of urban sprawl. She had stayed in Fresno once before when she was a child. Her foster mom's sister lived there and they had stayed the night on their way to vacation in Yosemite when Emily was a child. Her aunt lived on a narrow street with leafy trees, forming a tunnel, and Emily liked Fresno and her aunt very much, a high school teacher, who lived alone. Her house was full of books, books everywhere, even in boxes in the garage. Emily liked the neighborhood. She chose Fresno. Now she was working on her Master's in Social Work and she owned her own house.

She was looking through a window of her house at the apple tree on the lawn. "My boss hates me. I know he does," she said "I mean, lately."

I walked up next to her and looked out the window, too.

"Sounds like he's getting nervous suddenly that you know who you are for once in your life."

"What do you mean by that?" she asked.

"You're Indian now, of course he's going to hate you. Cowboys and Indians, get it?"

"I was Native American before I met you," she said.

"Yeah, but now you're an Indian," I said.

"You're crazy," she said.

"I'm serious. White people don't mind you looking Indian, but don't act it."

"You're being a bit over zealous, Freddy. Meaning you're . . ."

"I know what over zealous means, Emily."

"I'm sorry," she said. "Mr. Beauchamp used to really like me. We used to . . . Oh, I guess it doesn't matter."

"You used to what?" I said.

"Never mind," she said. "It's irrelevant."

"What's irrelevant? Tell me what you're talking about."

She turned around, the sun sitting on her shoulders like a little pet. "Nothing. I shouldn't have said anything."

"You're hiding something," I said.

"I don't want to talk about this." She walked away.

"You dated the Marlboro Man, didn't you? You fucking dated him."

"Don't talk to me like that."

"Did you sleep with him?"

"How dare you even ask," she said. "Have I ever asked who you slept with?"

"Fine," I said. "Don't tell me about your affair with John Wayne."

I looked at the apple tree, the street, the neighbor's small homes—and more trees up and down the street. Yellow leafs covered lawns, sidewalks, and some parked cars.

I put my arms around her. "You got nice trees in this neighborhood," I said. "I think I'm falling in love with . . . With your neighborhood."

She turned around. "You know, I got this house for such a good price," she said. "In LA this place would go for hundreds of thousands. I'm serious." She turned around and looked out the window. "But I guess this is supposed to be a bad neighborhood, huh? I mean, I guess it is one—although no one's tried to bother me. The neighbors I've met are good people. Sometimes I hear gun shots at night. But that's pretty normal, I guess. I mean, for living in a city, huh? I mean, for Fresno."

"Sure, neighbors kill each other all the time."

"May sound crazy," she said. "But I like this city. I'm never going to leave it."

"You found your homeland," I said.

"What about you, Freddy?"

"What about me?"

"You scare me," she said.

"Scare you?"

"Where are you going with your life?"

I was sitting in the cafeteria eating something Emily made. She cooked a few meals a week and took them to work and school as lunch, so she could save money by not eating out every day, and lately she had been giving me food to take too. When I told her I had nothing to save for, she assured me that I did, that I had a future that she was convinced was inevitable and dynamic, that I was too smart to not some day see the importance of an education. Today I had some sort of hamburger casserole, and it was pretty damn good compared to that frozen shit I used to eat everyday.

As I ate, I kept looking toward the entrance, waiting for Peacock, expecting him to come in. It was almost halfway into lunch and he hadn't appeared. People were finished eating and were leaving the cafeteria, going outside to smoke. Suddenly, an argument broke out on the other side of the cafeteria, but I couldn't tell what it was about because they were yelling at each other in Spanish, waving their arms close to each other's faces. Then one charged the other, pushing him back and they were fighting. The people sitting with them didn't do anything, they just watched. It was slow, each of the men trying to land a punch, and then stepping back as if to see if they had done any damage. It was as if they didn't really want to fight, but what else was there to do? They had no more words.

So the Mexicans articulated themselves, dancing in slow motion as their friends watched. Then a Sikh in an off-white turban walked up to one of the guys, gently put his hands on his shoulders and led him away, speaking to him softly in the ear. The other Mexican guy stormed out of the building.

I called Emily before lunch was over. "Freddy?" she said, surprised to hear from me.

"Yeah. What are you doing?" I said.

"Studying. Is something wrong?"

"No. I just called to say something."

"What is it, Freddy?"

"Well, see Emily. You know I'm in love with you, right? I mean, that's pretty obvious, isn't it?"

"Oh, Freddy, that's nice. Really, that's nice."

She said it like she meant it, not like she was brushing me off.

"I can't wait to see you," I said. "I'll come over right after work."

"Can't tonight. Sorry, baby. Tomorrow, okay, Freddy?'

"I thought we were going to . . ."

"My boss called. He wants me tonight. Sorry."

"He wants you, huh?"

"Don't start, Freddy."

He was already drunk when I got to the car after work. As I drove toward The Silver Spike, he handed me a bottle of tequila, half empty, and I took some gulps, waiting, waiting for the feeling to rise from the warmth in my stomach to the buzzing in my head. Peacock was irritating me, slurring about how tonight he was going to kick some ass. What bothered me was the way he emphasized his words by slapping his palms on the dashboard. What bothered me was that his wedding ring was off, and all that was left of it was a band of white skin, lighter than the rest of the finger. What bothered me were his eyes, because no matter what he was saying or doing, they were sad. I was quiet. I gulped. The more he talked, the angrier I got. At him. At the Marlboro Man. I drank more. My eyes focused on the road ahead of me.

"Those fuckers fired me," he said, slapping his palms on the dashboard. "Those fucks."

"What the hell did you expect, stupid? You were pulling heads off the chickens."

"It's a fucking chicken plant," he said. *"That's what we do."*

"Would you shut the hell up," I said.

He looked at me, swayed in drunkenness, closed one eye and scrutinized me with the other. "Are you talking to me?'

I took a big swig from the bottle. "No shit."

Then he yelled, poking his chest with his fat finger, making a thumping sound. "Me? You're talking like that to me?"

I could see the Marlboro Man in my head, putting his hand on Emily's waist, sliding it down further and further. I took another gulp.

"I'll kick your ass," Peacock said to me.

"Fuck you," I said, driving closer and closer to The Silver Spike. "I'd like to see you try it."

Aztlán, Oregon

When white people in Portland stared at Ben Chavez as if they had never seen a Mexican, it pissed him off. He had fantasies about coldcocking them, feeling their noses explode on his fist. Pulling open the doors of the Cafe del Cielo and walking in, sure enough, a white boy with round glasses and a head shaped like a pencil looked up from his book at Ben. It didn't occur to him that the guy might have recognized him from TV.

Mara Solorio sat in the corner reading a newspaper. She too looked up at Ben, who now stood across from her.

"Aren't you getting coffee?" she said.

"No, I'm fine," he said.

"Are you sure?"

"Really. I'm fine. Maybe we can go somewhere else."

She neatly folded up the newspaper.

"Where do you wanna go?"

"I don't know. I guess this place is fine."

Reluctantly he sat.

"Somebody's been asking about you, Ben," she said, pushing away a plate with a half-eaten blueberry muffin. "But before I tell you about it, you have to promise me two things. Two things, Ben, promise two things. Okay?"

"Are you going to eat that?"

"No, you want it? Two things: One, you listen to my advice without getting defensive. Two, nobody knows that I told you this. You gotta promise that. Ben, are you listening?"

Ben noticed that she'd taken only two or three bites of the muffin.

"So you're just going to waste it?" he said.

At fourteen he had learned not to waste food. One afternoon, he had plopped an egg into the pan, but the yoke broke, so he dumped it into the garbage and tried with a new egg. Looking up, he noticed his father's figure blocking the doorway. "Why did you throw that away?" his father asked.

A TV sitcom blared in the living room.

"I wanted it sunny side up. I like dipping the tortilla in the yoke." He was certain that his father who loved to eat would understand.

"What?" His chest expanded.

"The yoke broke."

"You threw away an egg because the yoke broke?"

"I wanted it sunny side up."

"Who the fuck you think you are, boy? A Rock-in-feller?" He stepped into the kitchen and raised a fist.

"I'm sorry," Ben said, shielding his head with his arms, stepping on the edge of the water pan underneath the fridge, spilling slimy water on the floor.

"Do you wanna buy the eggs from now on? Huh?" He tightened his lips around straight, white teeth, teeth that were not his own. His own had been knocked out in a bar fight.

"I'm sorry, Dad."

"I oughta hang you by your balls!"

"I just wanted an egg."

Mr. Chavez looked into the garbage and saw three of them, splattered with grease on the side of the brown, paper bag. "How the hell many did you waste?"

"I'm a lousy cook."

He saw the floor rising. Heard the laugh-track laughing. When he woke, he was on his bed, his mother holding a damp towel to his head.

"Are you okay?" she asked.

"Where is he?"

"Watching TV," she said.

"It ain't right what he did," he said.

"What'd *you* do?"

"I cooked an egg. That's all."

"And for that your father wants to kill you? Are you sure you're not leaving out some detail?"

"I like 'em sunny side up. That's the only way I like 'em. Well . . . sometimes I like 'em scrambled, but I wanted them sunny side up today. He must have hit me pretty hard."

"I heard it from the front yard."

He sat up on his bed. "I forgive him. Don't be mad at him, okay? I think I'll go watch *Starsky and Hutch* now."

"I wouldn't if I were you. He's likely to hit you again."

"Now wait a minute. If I'm willing to forget about it . . ."

"You must have done something. He gets carried away, but he's not cruel. What did you do?"

He told her.

"You little shit, how could you waste food like that?"

Now Mara's muffin made him angry. When Ben had been hired by the station, he had made it clear to his boss, Brad Myers, that he couldn't feel comfortable unless there were some brown people around, so Brad hired her, Hispanic token number two. Ben believed that the only differences between her and the white people were her accent and last name. Her rich family from Nicaragua had fled to the U. S. before the revolution in 1979. Her skin was the color of weak tea, and her eyes were blue. On Sunday nights when he anchored the news, she directed. She was brilliant because she saw everything through a camera. When she looked in Ben's eyes, even if she smiled and said something personal, he saw a director looking at him.

Whatever she wanted now, it wasn't personal.

"The network's looking for a station to host the 24-hour news," she said. Her pony-tail lay across her shoulder.

He pulled the muffin toward him and took a bitter bite.

"They're thinking about Portland. It'll run from two a.m. to five. They're talking about you as a possible anchor. This is national, Ben. Not all affiliates, but a lot of them."

"Who told you this?"

"Remember. Nobody knows you know this."

"Who told you?"

"Okay, here's the thing, Ben. Now take this as concern, okay?"

"Brad told you, right?" He resented the way she and the boss got along so well.

"I care about your future with the station. You're letting yourself go. You have to watch it."

"What do you mean?"

She sipped her coffee. "Physically, Ben. You're getting . . . chubby."

"I'm not chubby."

"You're chubby, Ben."

"You're crazy. I mean . . ."

"Look at your gut, Ben. Look down and see your gut. The camera sees that. You know, the camera adds to it. You're getting fat."

"Now it's fat?"

"Deny it if you want, fine, but not for too much longer or the network is going to pass you up. Ben, one of the things they're going to consider is your physical appearance."

With both palms he touched his face. "Are my cheeks getting fat?"

"Your cheeks *are* fat, Ben."

"Oh, my God. I didn't even notice."

"Life's been good to you."

"I mean, I don't care. I mean, who cares what I look like ultimately, you know?"

"Well, the network cares. I care because if you blow this deal, you blow it for me too."

"That's not fair."

"That's the way it is. Listen, it shouldn't take you long. Spend some time at the gym, start eating right. The station is sending tapes of you to the network. They want recent ones, and frankly, Ben, we don't have a lot of great stuff lately. It's like your enthusiasm is draining. Let's do some good features next week, something that shows you off. I have some ideas. Do you want to hear them?"

"Whatever."

"Hispanic street gangs. This of course has been done before, but by people too out of touch with the streets to dig deep. But you. Didn't you used to be in a gang in California?"

"Something like that."

When they walked to her car, Ben looked into the eyes of the white men he passed on the sidewalk, as if daring them to mad-dog him, but the one man that did look at him smiled, and Ben couldn't help but smile back. They were everywhere in Portland. He got so lonely that he would drive around towns where some Mexican farmworkers lived, Woodburn, Gervais, Independence, sometimes stopping in cafes or pubs. At these times, he never said anything, he just sipped his coffee or beer, looked straight ahead, and listened to their Spanish, trying to guess by their accents which part of Mexico they came from: Jalisco, Michoacán, Guerrero.

"You going to be all right?" Mara asked, unlocking the door to her Corolla.

"Of course," he said. "I was just thinking how much I hate this town."

"Too white for you?"

"Yeah, that's it."

"You're such a racist," she said.

"But for the good side."

"Really, Ben. You need to get over it. Before you do something stupid."

She got in and drove off. He watched her car disappear in traffic, and he ate the rest of her muffin.

In high school, his teachers hated him. They judged him because he dressed like a *cholo:* baggy pants, crisp white T-shirts, and work boots. One woman requested that he be transferred from her English class before she even read his writing. By the time he was a senior, now a leader in his gang, he was used to it. He attended school more for his personal amusement, he believed, than a desire to get educated, and he began to enjoy living up to their expectations of him. Mr. Shell hated him the most. He was the civics teacher, and from the first day he was short with Ben, threatening him with expulsion when he laughed at the wrong moment or said something the rest of the class thought was funny. Mr. Shell didn't like that the students in class—the Chicanos at least—paid more attention to Ben than to him.

The students were required to volunteer four hours a semester working for a presidential campaign. Ben didn't like any of the candidates, so he wanted to work with an old radical named Marta Banuelos who had a platform telling white people to go back to Europe and leave Aztlán to the Indians. Mr. Shell, a bald man with sad eyes and sagging cheeks, said no, that Ben had to work for a legitimate candidate.

"Anderson doesn't have a chance at being elected," Ben argued in class. "Yet to you he's a legitimate candidate? Could it be because he's white?"

"Yeah," a few Chicanos in class murmured.

"I'm not required to explain myself to you," Mr. Shell said.

"Well you better tell me why."

"Or what?" Mr. Shell said, dropping his roll book on his desk with a thud and walking closer to Ben. "Or what, Ben? Are you threatening me?"

"Lighten up, old man. I just wanna know."

"I'm the teacher here. Not you."

Suddenly a white girl from the front of the class raised her hand and said Mr. Shell's name.

"What?" he answered.

"Why can't he work for whomever he wants?" she asked.

"Well, uh, this Banuelos person sounds like a protest candidate."

"So what's your point?" Ben asked.

"Okay, Ben, go ahead, I don't care."

When Marta Banuelos—who looked like Ben's *abuelita*—drove him through the neighborhood behind the Veteran's Hospital, he told her no Mexicans lived there, just retired white people. He knew, he said, because his mother worked at the hospital.

"Brown people are everywhere," she said in Spanish, hunched over her steering wheel, her face old. She dropped him off in front of a chain-link fence surrounding the hospital parking lot.

As he walked by the tiny homes and duplexes, he read the names on the mailboxes. One box carved from wood said, "Godishere." He thought that was an interesting name, but they weren't Mexicans, so he didn't go to the door and knock.

He walked across the hospital lawn through the parking lot where a fat security guard looked at him suspiciously. Ben walked cool, *cholo* style, his legs in front, his upper body falling behind, as if he were kicking back, and he had a tattoo on his forearm that said NSF, North Side Fresno. He was aware that the fat security guard was following him, so he walked like he owned the damn place down the ramp to emergency, through the automatic doors, past a man screaming on the floor surrounded by nurses and held down by orderlies. He pushed through double doors into a hallway where moans mixed with machine noises, typewriters, a toilet flushing, and his soles sweeping the floor.

The double doors at the end opened onto a large bright room with orange couches, and TV sets braced on the walls. Alicia Chavez, behind the counter on a stool, was talking in Spanish to an old nun. The nun left the counter, Ben approached it. "Are you registered to vote?" he asked his mother.

"Did I forget something at home?" she said.

"No. I was canvassing the neighborhood."

Her line rang. She told him to hold on and started talking, checking information from filing cabinets and reading it over the phone. He waited on one of the orange couches across from the TV and watched a soap opera. The volume was too low to hear it over the sound of patients moaning and coughing. Through the double doors, the fat security guard walked in, looked around, spotted Ben and walked over to him. "What are you doing here?" he said, attempting to sound intimidating, although to Ben he sounded like a little boy trying to be tough. Ben ignored him.

Alicia came up and said hi to the security guard and introduced them. "Ben," she said. "This is Roy. Roy, this is my son."

"I heard a lot about you, son." Suddenly Roy was friendly and animated, and sincerely so. He shook Ben's hand heartily. "So you make sculptures from clay? I hear your dragon won first prize at the fair."

"That's his brother," Alicia said. "This is the one that wants to be a movie star."

"Used to," Ben wanted to say, because now it sounded so childish to admit what his dreams had been.

"You're the one that reads those detective novels?" Ben asked.

"Why, yes," Roy said, surprised and pleased that he should know something about him. "I love reading."

He wanted to tell Roy to quit giving them to his mother. They were all over the house, and he picked them up sometimes and read them. In one, some sleuth was on an airplane over the California coast with a Mexican pilot, who turned out to be one of the bad guys. He said to the hero, "*Señor*, I theenk your time she is up," and he tried to push him out of the plane, but a struggle ensued and the Mexican got pushed out instead. "*Adios, amigo,*" said the hero as he watched the Mexican drop.

Roy told Alicia he had to get back to the parking lot. "Bye, Ben," he said, shaking his hand again. They both watched him waddle away.

"You have to get back, I guess?" she asked.

"I guess."

"Ben?"

"Yeah?"

"Do you still want to be an actor?"

"I don't think so."

"What do you want to do?"

"I don't know."

"Maybe you should be on the news. An anchorman."

"Why do you say that?"

"You have to do something that shows off that handsome face of yours."

"Whatever."

When Banuelos picked him up, he told her that everyone slammed doors in his face. Next she dropped him off in the barrio on a street lined with houses and apartment buildings. He got out and started walking.

Here he is, he thought, ace reporter wandering the way of Aztlán, *con los Chicanos, la gente*, seeking the stories behind the headlines. He would go deeper and deeper, to the roots of the people's problems.

Three *cholos,* gang members, stood in front of their car across the street, their music so loud the bass beat with his heart. They stared at him, and his knees went weak because he was banging from another barrio, so they would assume he was disrespecting them. This was a death sentence, especially with his shining North Side tattoo. The three crossed the street, coming at him, one of them huge, built like a bulldog, with a flannel shirt untucked and buttoned at the top, *cholo* style.

"Where you from, eh?" the big one said.

Ben nodded greetings. "North Side," he said.

"What you doing in our barrio?"

"Yeah, *ese,* we oughtta slice you," said a short skinny kid, not more than fourteen, who kept one hand in his pocket. To get away clean, Ben knew he could knock the big guys down and run, but he wouldn't know where the kid was. He would just know to expect a sharp blade cutting and slicing from all sides until his clothes were soaked with blood.

He took two steps back. "Listen, *vatos,* I don't mean no disrespect to your barrio. I'm campaigning for Banuelos. She's a Chicana, man, running for president."

With one hand in his pocket, he grasped the handle of his knife, just in case.

He told them that *gabachos* had been running Aztlán since they took it from Mexico in 1848. Even before that, he explained, the Europeans of Mexico ran the lives of Indians, of brown people. And today things are just as bad. He gave them a few examples of injustices he had seen in his own barrio, police brutality, poverty, hard-working Chicanos accused of being lazy. They nodded their heads.

As long as other people ran things, he said, Chicanos were always going to be fighting each other. Even though they didn't have a chance in winning the national election, the process, he said, was a means of unification. Even if only for a moment, he said, we need to come together and acknowledge who the enemy truly is. He went on and on and at some point he ceased to know what he was saying; all he knew was that he was using words to do the one thing he had to do: survive.

Giving him the Chicano handshake, they said he could stay, and they even pointed out houses of people they knew. "If they give you any problem about being in the neighborhood, just tell them 'F 14' sent you."

When the elections were over, Ben turned in an essay on the importance of the Banuelos campaign to Chicano unity, an historical perspective. One day Mr. Shell held the report in his hands. To the surprise of everyone in the class, he said, "This is the best paper I've ever read on this assignment, Ben. This is college-level work. I hope you're going to college, Ben."

He looked into the turtle eyes of the teacher. "I was thinking of majoring in journalism," he said.

Twenty-four-hour news. It was a start. But to what? Where would he wind up? The Chicano Walter Cronkite? When he arrived at his condo after meeting with Mara, he was both excited and depressed. He hated himself, but he didn't know why. He picked up the phone and called home. His father answered. "Yeah?"

"Hey, Dad."

"Junior?"

"No, Dad, the other one."

"Hey, hey, the reporter. Benny boy!"

"How you doing?" Ben asked.

"Your dumb brother got beat up again. Third time in three months."

"Is he all right?"

"Yeah. Just a little bruised."

"How'd it happen?"

"Pulled him out of his car this time. You still got that Cadillac?"

"It's a Honda. Yeah, I still got it."

"How much did that thing cost?"

"Eighteen."

"Hundred?"

"Thousand," Ben said.

"Woo. Bought this house for less than that," his father said. "You should be buying property with your money. Don't be an idiot all your life."

"Guess what, Dad?" He wanted to say something dramatic, like,

"I'm going to be famous," but he couldn't say anything about it, in case it didn't come true. He found himself saying, "I'm coming home. I have a week's vacation coming up."

"Yeah. So, why are you spending it here? I thought you went to Europe for your vacations."

"That was only once."

"How much did you spend on that vacation?"

"I don't remember."

"More than I paid for my Oldsmobile, I'll bet."

"Anyway, I'm coming home."

"Why?"

"I need to be with family."

His father understood that. "When you coming home?"

"I could probably drive out there in a few weeks. Where's Ma?"

"She went to get Junior. He was in the drive-thru at Arby's. Wanted to get a sandwich."

"You sure he's okay?"

"Yeah, yeah."

"Okay, Pop. Expect me, huh? I'll be seeing you."

"Okay. Bye."

"Bye."

He heard himself say "Pop." He had never used that word before. Pop.

Why didn't he speak Spanish with his father? Was he getting rusty? Plenty of white people in Portland spoke it, but what was the point when they could talk more easily in English? In fact, every time some white person tried to talk to him in Spanish, it pissed him off, although he wasn't sure why.

He flicked on the lights in the hallway and saw his full-body reflection in the mirror at the end. Walking closer, he got bigger and bigger until he stood in front of himself. He pulled off his shirt and tossed it on the floor. His pants dropped. His thighs were fat. And his waist: Fat.

He *was* getting fat. Fighting for his people is what he used to be about, but ever since he'd been away from Aztlán, all he took care of was himself.

Stepping out of his underwear, he picked up the phone to call

Mara's home.

"Guess what I'm doing?"

"Why are you talking Spanish?"

"Guess what I'm—"

"I don't know."

"Looking at myself. You were right."

"You see it?"

"I do."

He asked her to arrange a vacation, but she said it was impossible. The network hadn't made their final decision.

"Come on, Mara, please."

"You do want this, don't you?"

"I do. I want it."

"I'll tell you what," she said in English. "Let's do something substantial first, something we can show the network, something that shows not only how smart you are, but how good you look. They're also considering an African-American woman in Phoenix. You can have your vacation later. Have you thought about any of the ideas?"

"I like the gang thing," he said.

"Let's drive around tomorrow, you know, through the gang neighborhoods."

"The angle might be radical," he warned. "Tell it like it is. I know in *Califas*, most of those gang members are pretty political. They know what's going on. And the fact is, they don't like white people."

"Any way you want."

"I want . . ."

He wanted to get there early. He followed the click of her heels. She pulled keys from her coat pocket, and whispered, "Be patient."

She didn't need to be there, he told her.

"I want to be there," she said, flicking on the lights of her office. After checking her messages and returning one call, she said, "Okay, let's go," but then she stopped again to drink from a water cooler, and he wondered if she was trying to make him angry, as if she knew that somewhere on the streets of Portland was his answer, his reason for being so far from Aztlán, so far away.

Before they could get out of the studio, the station manager, Brad

Myers, walked up to them. "Hi, Ben," he said, smiling big. Although in his late thirties, Brad looked like a twelve-year-old boy dressed up in his father's suit.

As Brad and Mara stood there, Ben walked down the hall to a couch. He sat and waited while they spoke in hushed voices, and he could make out what they were saying.

Brad: "What did he do when you told him he was fat?"

Mara: "What could he do?"

Ben grabbed a fistful of flab above his belt.

Then he heard a voice calling from outside. At the end of the hallway stood Mara. "Come on, Ben," she said, holding the door open, sunlight coming through. "Let's get going."

They drove through narrow streets lined with shabby homes and corner stores. They spotted a small group of teenage Chicanos dressed like gang members hanging around on the sidewalk in front of a brick building.

"That's them," he said, pulling the van to the curb.

"Be careful," she said.

"You mean *they* better be careful," he said.

He got out of the van to greet them, but they weren't looking at him. They looked at Mara. So he looked too.

Watched her step out of the van.

She smiled at everyone, wondering why all the attention was on her.

Ben approached the homies. "Wuz happening?" he asked.

They looked him up and down, then they looked back at Mara. One of the boys had flaring nostrils and he was tall, dark, and thin; and as he leaned against the brick wall, he looked at Ben with suspicious eyes, and said, "What you want, man?"

Ben guessed he was the leader.

"*Orale!* That's Ben Chavez, man. The *vato* on the news," said one of the gangsters, a small guy with a skinny face and shoulder-length hair that curled like Geri curls.

"That's right," Ben said. "What's your name?" he asked the leader.

"What you want, man?"

"He wants to interview us, I betcha, homes. Huh, ain't that right?

You're doing a story on gangs and shit, huh?"

"Chicano street gangs," he confirmed.

"*Chale*, man. I don't want to be interviewed," said the leader.

Ben felt the gold watch heavy on his wrist, the neck tie tight around his collar. "Listen, *ese*," he said, removing his tie and stuffing it in his pocket. I'm from the barrio, too. *Serio.* I'm from *Califas*. Involved in the same damn shit. I wanna tell it like it is. White people don't know shit about us. I understand why you guys are in gangs, man. It's this *pinche* society, *verdad?* Brown people don't have a chance in this white, racist society."

The leader looked at Mara then back at Ben. "What the fuck are you talking about?" He turned around and entered the building.

The guy with curls stood alone as his homeboys filed into the building behind the tall boy. "Hey, man don't pay no attention to Rafa, man. He hates everyone. *¿Sabes?* But I'll talk to you, man. I tell you everything, eh. When's this coming on TV and shit?"

Ben looked to Mara. "Get the camera," he said, entering the building.

The dim room was lit by the lights above the pool tables and the screens of video games. An Asian woman sat on a stool behind a bar where soft drinks and cigarettes were sold. Some of the boys were setting up a game of pool, Rafa sitting on a wooden chair against the wall, his legs extended, arms crossed, like a hoodlum bored in class. Behind him pool cues hung on a wooden rack.

Ben undid his watch as they watched, tossed it on the middle of their pool table, and rolled up his sleeves, exposing his tattoo. Rafa looked up at him, shaking his head slowly. "You're crazy, man."

"Listen," Ben said. "I don't know what impression you have of me, but I'm just a Chicano, all right? I mean no disrespect to your barrio, all right? I'm here because I need to tell your story. Please, let me tell your story."

Mara said it was the best interview Ben had ever done. They followed Rafa home, to school, out with his gang, and one night behind an abandoned building, they got some footage of his gang in a fight with an African-American gang. The report took a week to complete. Mara said that what Rafa talked about was wise and sad and naive all at once, a real testimony to society. It was a great piece.

Ben hated it.

He had wanted it to say something radical, but when Rafa got to the heart of what *he* wanted to say, Ben didn't want to hear it. Rafa had a dream of owning a house, having a wife and kids and "nice things." He had no consciousness of a political struggle, no concept of the Chicano Movement. He didn't even know who Ché was. Rafa said that if he could go to college he would want to major in business. He could see himself as a businessman, "making all kinds of money and shit." Whenever Ben tried to get what he thought of society into the interview—whenever he suggested that it was racist and responsible for the condition of Chicanos—Rafa looked at him funny, looked at Mara, and back to Ben. "Well, I don't know about that," Rafa would say, "but . . ." and he'd continue saying things that hurt Ben to hear.

After Mara had taken the footage for editing, she called him and told him to come see it. He hadn't eaten at all that day because it didn't occur to him to eat. He was pacing his condo, naked, back and forth, faster and faster, full of energy but with no way to expend it. The curtains and windows were open, the cold breeze flowing through.

"Brad wants to see it too," she said.

"You can watch it together. I'm staying home."

"Come on, Ben, be there. It really looks good. I'm serious. This is the best feature on gangs I've ever seen. Come see it. It'll blow you away."

He walked past the security desk of the station. He walked down the hallway to the viewing rooms and entered a door. Mara and Brad quit talking and looked at Ben. "Hi, Ben," Brad said.

The room was small with a large video monitor.

Ben sat down and looked at the screen. Mara started the tape. It ran for four minutes, each minute more and more painful to him, full of things he hated. When the tape was over, he felt like picking up the monitor and throwing it across the room.

"My God, Ben! That was incredible," said Brad.

The voice grated on him like a shovel on hardpan.

"Excellent. Excellent," Brad continued. "Ben, let me shake your hand."

Brad appeared in front of him, a sickeningly sincere look on his face, his hand extended. "Oh, Ben, the network's going to love this. And you look good in this piece. That coat compliments you."

"What do you mean by that?"

"You look good, that's all," he said, patting Ben on the shoulder, looking at Mara and smiling.

"Don't touch me," Ben said. "What the fuck do you mean that coat compliments me?"

"Er . . ." Brad looked at Mara.

"Don't look at her, I'm talking to you. You think I'm too fat?"

"Ben," Mara said, putting her hand on his shoulder.

"Stay out of this." Then he looked into Brad's face. "You think I'm too fat?"

"Ben, I don't like this," Brad said.

"Of course you don't like it, stupid, I'm about to kick your ass."

He didn't remember the first hit to Brad's stomach, but somewhere he must have been thinking of holding back most of his rage because he didn't hurt him as bad as he could have. He didn't break his legs or kill him. He simply punched his body with a *thud thud thud* like in the movies, again and again.

Mexican Table

Members of Mr. Benard's eleventh-grade Beginning Comp class, one by one, told him which English course they were taking in the fall. I sat at the back of the room, my legs stretched under the small desk. I was stoned again, having smoked out on the long walk to school. When the word came to me, I said "Popular Fiction," a class I knew would be easy.

"No!" Mr. Benard yelled, shaking his curly head, waving his hands in the air. "You're too smart for that, Willy. Take Intermediate Comp. Take me again."

I was surprised he would say this to me after I had only been in his class for three weeks, and so were the other students, who looked back at me as if seeing me for the first time. I didn't look like a good student. I had my hair long and un-styled, way past my shoulders, my eyes were always half shut, and I was one of the few non-whites at Bullard High. Most of the students were rich kids, most of them what everyone called "socies." They wore nice clothes, got expensive haircuts, and drove new cars. Although my sister was poor, her apartment was built years before the development had come, in a small neighborhood surrounded by fig orchards and separated from the nice houses by a freeway. When I moved in with her, I ended up in the Bullard district.

Mr. Benard said, for all the students to hear, that I owe it to such and such concept or symbol to excel in school, being that I'm smart.

"I used to teach on the east side of town, so I know what I'm talking about," he said, pointing his finger at me.

The east side was where the Chicanos lived.

When class was over, all the students blurred through the door and into the sunlight. I went up to Mr. Benard's desk and asked what time he offered the Comp class.

"I'm not teaching it next year," he said, standing by his chair, pulling his glasses off his long nose and blowing on the lenses. "But I want you to sign up for my fourth-period Basic Reading."

"That's Bonehead English," I said. "Stoners take that so they won't have to write papers. "

"I want to be able to work closely with you, Willy. You're smart. While all the boneheads are doing their reading, you and I'll sit down and work on your writing."

"But why should I work that hard if I'm just going to get Basic Reading credit?"

"Don't worry," he said. "It'll come out on your report card as Intermediate Comp. I'll get it cleared with the principal. Trust me."

I spent that summer living with Sally, my 21-year-old sister, in her second floor apartment next to the freeway. She worked swing shift at a donut shop, and I worked a few hours a day with an Okie guy named Earl who lived down the street. He fixed washers and dryers in his garage and paid me cash. I would hand him tools while he listened to country music and told racist Mexican jokes. One time he stuck his head out from the belly of a washing machine and said, "You don't mind them Mexican jokes, do you?"

"Yeah, I do," I said.

"Well, hell, *amigo*," he said, "I won't tell them no more."

After that he told Mongolian jokes, but it was clear they were still about Mexicans.

Why do Mongolians have those little steering wheels in their lowriders?

So they can drive with handcuffs on.

By the time I got home each day, Sally was leaving for work, so I only saw her on weekends or nights I stayed up late reading or watching the small black and white TV we had on the carpet in the middle of the nearly bare living room. At around midnight, when headlights flashed through the golden drapes, I would go outside and stand under the porch light until she got into the apartment. On weekends we went to the movies and shopped for groceries, and some Saturday nights I took her little Plymouth Duster and went alone to a teen dance club called The Electra, where I used to meet girls, the only human contact I had other than Sally and Earl. In the evenings, while Sally worked, I had nothing to do, no school, no friends, so I spent my time reading books I had bought at a nearby secondhand store, everything from Sidney Sheldon to Shakespeare.

One hot afternoon I was reading at the table while my sister was preparing her lunch, scooping fruit salad into a Tupperware bowl. "Maybe you could clean the apartment today," she said. Her thick, black Indian hair hung to the middle of her back. She put her Tupperware into a bag and rolled it closed. I went back to my book until I felt her eyes on me.

"You're a good student, aren't you?" she asked. "I mean, a lot better than I was. Have you ever thought about college?"

"Not too much," I said.

She grabbed her purse from the table. "I'm serious," she said. "I've read your papers when you leave them on the table." She headed for the front door, reached for the handle, and turned around. "I could never write like that."

"My English teacher said I was too smart for 'Popular Fiction.' He wants me to take Intermediate Comp."

"I can see why," she said.

She opened the door, and sunlight shot in.

"Maybe over the summer you could give me writing assignments," I said. "I'm losing practice."

"Maybe over the summer you could keep the apartment clean," she said, walking into the sun.

Two weeks before the end of this long, boring summer, I went outside to check the mail. I got my class schedule, which said that for fourth period, I was signed up for Mr. Benard's Basic Reading.

I tried to explain to him—while stoners with rock and roll T-shirts and leather purses passed into the door—that my class schedule said Basic Reading and not Intermediate Composition.

"Oh, I know," he said. "You'll be getting Intermediate Comp credit. Don't worry about it."

I went to sit in the back of the class.

"No," he demanded, loud enough to startle and quiet the entire class. "Don't sit with *them,* Willy." Then he said to the class, "Willy's not taking Basic Reading. He's taking Intermediate Comp. He'll be in class the same time as the rest of you, but he'll be doing work a lot harder than what you guys have to do. He'll be writing."

Members of the class looked at me through long hair and red eyes. I recognized in the back of the room a boy named Andy. Before summer, I'd had him in P.E. He had shoulder-length brown hair and glasses, and he was big, chubby, tall, and strong. I had seen him teasing one of his friends by lifting him up over his head and spinning him around. Once during P.E. roll call, while the boys lined up against a cement wall, Andy looked me up and down.

"Hey, Guerra," he said. "The Mexican section is over there." He pointed to the end of the line where the only other two Chicanos were standing. "Why don't you go over there and join your people." He laughed and looked into the eyes of the guy next to him, another stoner. That guy laughed too.

Now Andy was eyeing me from the back row of the class.

Mr. Benard told me to sit at a table in front of the room where another student was sitting, a Mexican girl. She had black wavy hair with a pink bow. Her dress, pink and white, was the kind little girls used to wear in grade school. She looked shy in front of the class, head down, afraid to look up. I sat across from her and was going to say "hi" but she didn't look up, so I left her alone.

Mr. Benard shut the students up and explained that they would pick a book from the shelf and spend class time reading. When the bell rang, they had to put it back. Every time they finished a book, they would get a questionnaire, stacked on his desk. Then they would answer questions about what they read. After addressing the class, he came to our table and introduced me to the girl.

Her name was Pilar.

"Hello, how are you?" she said to me, in a thick Mexican accent.

"I'm Willy," I said. "Willy Guerra."

"Isn't Guerra the Spanish word for *war*?" Mr. Benard asked, pushing his glasses up his nose.

Suddenly someone yelled from the back of the room. We all looked and saw Andy arguing with another stoner guy. Andy held a book behind his back, while the other guy tried to grab it.

"You better give it to me," the guy said.

"What are you going to do about it?" Andy said.

Mr. Benard stood up from our table and walked over there. "What's going on here?" he said.

"I found this first," said Andy, holding a copy of *The Brady Bunch: The Paperback.*

I looked at Pilar, who was doodling her name in the corner of her note pad. "Are you signed up for Intermediate Comp?"

"Beginning. You're intermediate?"

"Yeah, I guess," I said.

"I hate writing. I can write better in Spanish because in English I have problems with grammar. Do you know Spanish?"

"Not too good."

"Ay, Guillermo, and you a Mexican. You should be ashamed of yourself. *Eres Mexicano, ¿verdad?"*

"*Simón que* yes!" I said.

"Well, you should speak Spanish."

She smiled and winked, probably to let me know she was only kidding.

"Well, you're in America now, so you better start learning your grammar," I said.

"Will you help me?"

"Maybe," I said, realizing she wasn't as shy as she looked.

Mr. Benard came back and sat down. He gave us a copy of the first assignment, and then started explaining what it said, as if we couldn't read or something.

We were to pretend we had a cousin from another country coming to visit. What would we show him or her about being American? What kind of things would we do that represent what Americans do? As Mr. Benard talked, I thought about having someone visit me in Fresno. How would I show him a good time? What would we talk about? I thought about the last time my mom and dad were in town. They didn't even come to the apartment; they just went to my grand-mother's, visited and left. I guess they still hadn't forgiven me.

I'd take my long-lost cousin with me to the dance club. We'd meet girls together. We'd get stoned and laugh at stupid things.

"Give 'em back, you asshole," yelled a girl from the back of the room. Mr. Benard rose. Andy was in another argument, this time with the girl. I looked at Pilar, who was looking down at the assignment.

"Why did you take Mr. Benard?" I asked. "Why didn't you take a regular Comp class?"

"He asked me to," she said. "I have him last year for Basic Reading. He likes my work."

In the back of the room Mr. Benard stood in front of Andy, holding his hand out saying, "Give it to me now." Andy was about two feet taller than the teacher. Reluctantly, he put a pack of cigarettes in Mr. Benard's hand. Mr. Benard gave it back to the girl.

My mom called that night to ask how things were going with me and Sally.

"Ok," I said. I was standing on the balcony.

"Sally at work?"

"Yup."

Beyond the messy parking lot of the complex stood a ten-foot high chain-link fence, separating us from the freeway, which now was filled with cars zooming by, little dots of light streaming away.

"Well if you need anything, just call."

"I will," I said.

We said nothing for a while.

"I really like my English class," I said.

"That's nice."

"I was thinking of maybe going to college," I said.

"That'll be the day," she said.

After I hung up, I sat at the small dining room table to begin my essay. I decided to pretend I had a long-lost cousin from Mongolia, a place I knew nothing about. His name was Moochie, and I would teach him the finer points of American life.

Time With Moochie

When Moochie got off the jet liner, I recognized him immediately. He was more wrapped then he was dressed and he carried a big sign that said my name: WILLY GUERRA. I approached him, took off my sunglasses and said, "You must be Moochie."

"Who are you?" he asked in a thick Mongolian accent.

"Think about it," I said.

He thought.

"You are the pilot?" he asked. "Thank you for wonderful flight."

Mr. Benard had an announcement for the class. "We're going to have a student teacher from the university come in a few weeks. I want you guys to be extra nice. If I find out that any of you are in the slightest bit rude, I'll have you out of the classroom and out on the streets where you belong."

He told the class to start their reading, and then he came up to the table where Pilar and I sat with our chairs facing the rest of the class, as if we were his bailiffs.

"When the student teacher gets here, I'll have more time to spend with you people," he said. "Okay, pull out your papers."

Mine was about seven handwritten pages, and I handed it to Mr. Benard.

"Give it to Pilar," he said. "You're going to read each other's."

Hers was about her cousin Otilia coming to visit from Mexico. She wrote that one of the first things they would do is go shopping and they would buy a lot of "pretty outfits for Otilia to wear." Then they would go to school together, and Otilia would learn English. She would tell Otilia to watch out for American boys, that they were no good, rude and disrespectful, caring only for themselves. By the middle of the story, Otilia wanted desperately to go back to Mexico, with a desire that ached in her heart. But Otlia's father explained to them that there were no opportunities where they lived. They had to stay so he could work in the fields. Pilar was torn between being glad to have someone live with her and feeling pity for her cousin that she had to stay, too.

When I finished reading, all I could say was "wow." She expressed herself well. I watched her read the rest of mine. After she was done, she put it down and looked at me.

"Don't you have any cousins in Mexico?" she asked.

The bell rang for lunchtime. Pilar and I cleared our table and walked out together. We were behind the other students, right behind Andy, who looked back at us, shook his head in pity and said, "Enjoy your burritos." Students were crammed in the halls, laughing with each other, hitting each other playfully. Pilar said bye to me and walked off, disappearing in a blur of people.

A stoner kid, sitting on a green bench, held a Hostess fruit pie in one hand and a cigarette in the other. He took a bite from the pie, chewed it, and then took a drag of the cigarette, blew out the smoke, and bit from the pie again. He was doing it so quickly that it looked like he might get confused and accidentally take a drag of the pie and eat the cigarette. Four or five other stoners, one of them Andy, walked up to him. Andy grabbed the last half of the pie and gobbled it down in one bite. The guy yelled, "You're such an asshole, dude!"

Then Andy spotted me and smiled mischievously. I put my cigarette out and walked away. I went to watch the Chicano students play volleyball on the lawn between two buildings. Any group of students could form a team, and the Chicano students formed one. They seemed to beat just about everyone else. These guys were *cholos* from the east side, and they wore creased pants and white T-shirts. There were so few of them at Bullard that they could all fit on the same team.

I liked to watch them play, to see them nearly jumping over the net to spike the ball hard—the loud thump of their brown fists on the white ball—or yelling "I got it! I got it!" as it slowly descended on them like a silent bomb, and then slamming it—Thump!—into the farthest corner of the other team's territory. I imagined myself on their team. I wanted to be on their team. But I didn't know them.

He was wearing one of those beanies with a red propeller on top, and a plaid suit, the pants high watered, and pink socks. "I look cool, no? Chicks will dig me now."

"No, Moochie," I said. "Put the beanie away."

"Just watch this," he said, walking between packed tables to the edge of the dance floor where sat the most beautiful girl in the whole disco. Moochie bent over and extended his hand.

"Would you care to cut the jug?" he asked. "Trip the knight in plastic?"

She started laughing so hard that she bent over. The entire disco was watching now, and when they noticed Moochie's hat they too started laughing. All except for her boyfriend. He looked like he wanted to beat Moochie up.

"Why do they laugh?" Moochie asked me, with innocent brown eyes.

"Come on, Moochie," I said. "Let's get outta here."

Pilar and I were at the library doing research for our next paper. We were looking through the shelves of books, pulling things out and pushing them back in.

"Look at this," she said, holding a Colby book with photos of military jets. "You like jets?"

"I hate jets."

"Oh. I thought all little boys like jets," she said, smiling. I wasn't sure if she was serious or if she was teasing me.

I noticed a pretty white girl with a stack of books stepping up to the checkout counter. She smiled at the librarian when the old lady stamped her books and handed them back to her. She skipped out the double doors of the entrance into the sunlight. I was suddenly depressed.

"Mine's on drugs," said Pilar.

"No it's not. I was thinking about something else," I said.

"Where are you from?" she asked.

"Fremont. You probably never heard of it," I said. "It's in the Bay Area."

"*¿Cerca de San Francisco?*"

"*Más o menos.*"

"Oh." She looked down at the book in her hand. "My paper is on drugs. Do you know anything about drugs?"

After the bell rang, we left the library together, but I walked alone to the smoking section.

The smoking section, two rows of green picnic benches between the cafeteria and the administration building, was right in front of the principal's picture window. He stood now by his desk, looking out at us smokers. My first days at Bullard High, I had to suppress a reflex to hide my cigarette whenever he looked.

I noticed Andy watching me from a couple of benches away as he talked to his stoner friends. They all turned around and looked at me. Andy's mouth was moving and his friends were laughing. All of the sudden he yelled, "THAT'S RIGHT! MY ENGLISH CLASS HAS A MEXICAN TABLE!"

Other people sitting around the section laughed. The principal sat down in his chair and swiveled around, returning to his paperwork.

The next day Andy walked to the front of the class to grab a questionnaire on Mr. Benard's desk. "There's the Mexican table," he mumbled as he passed us. "Be careful things don't slide off."

I looked into his eyes, and he stopped and mad-dogged me, looking as if he'd like to hit me hard, but I didn't turn my gaze away until Pilar touched my arm with warm fingers. "It's okay," she said.

Andy walked back to his desk.

"That boy is bad," she said. *"Sinvergüenza."*

"If he wants to fight, I'll fight him," I said, under my breath, loud enough for only her to hear. Really I didn't want to fight him. All his friends would gather around and probably put in their jabs and kicks, too. Who would help me? Certainly not the Chicanos.

As part of our research paper, we had to write a survey for the students of Basic Reading to answer. The topic was teenagers and things that affected them. I was writing on television. Pilar was writing on drugs. As I was handing the survey to the stoners in class, Andy was talking to the guy at the desk next to him. I handed Andy a form.

"I won't be filling one out," he said.

"Why not?" I asked.

"I don't answer questions for Mexicans," he said.

I put one on his desk anyway. "Just do it."

"I told you I ain't doing it."

"You'll fill one out all right," said Mr. Benard from the front of the class. "And you'd better do it right."

While the rest of the class filled theirs out, Andy and I looked at each other, and he mouthed the words, "I'm going to kill you." With his finger he gestured a slit throat.

When we got the surveys back, I tried to guess which one was Andy's, and it wasn't hard. Under the question "How many hours of TV do you watch a day?" he wrote, "None of your dam bizzness greeser."

When I looked up, my eyes caught his, and he smiled big, clenching his fist. Later, when he was looking through the bookshelf near our table, I said to Pilar, loud enough for him to hear, "I guess some people weren't smart enough to understand the survey."

Immediately I regretted it. He came up to our table, leaned over, placing his big palms flat on the surface, and said, "I hope you know, Guerra, that I'm going to kick your ass."

"Oh, you're scaring me," I said, sarcastically, while inside my heart beat hard.

"You'll be dead, spik."

"Andy?" yelled Mr. Benard. "What are you doing?"

"Just telling these fine students how much I admire their smartness," he said, smiling evilly at me.

I was scared not only because Andy was bigger than me—bigger than anyone in school practically—but because I also knew he would make sure that he surrounded me with his friends, that no authorities could see him pulverize me inside the circle. I tried to pretend like I didn't take his threat seriously, but during lunch I stayed in the smoking section in the view of the principal's window. Andy paced around a bench watching me, mumbling threats, hitting with a thud his big fist into the palm of his hand.

Moochie was sad when we left the disco, walking with his head down. "I no do good, no?" he asked.

"Don't worry, Moochie," I said, patting him on the back. "No one's good at everything."

He smiled. The propeller on his beanie slowly spun.

"But take that stupid thing off!"

Before we could get across the parking lot, three big guys came after us, the tallest with long brown hair and glasses, the boyfriend of the girl Moochie tried to dance with.

"We're in trouble," I said. "Looks like they want to fight."

"So we fight," said Moochie calmly.

"You don't understand, Moochie. They're big suckers."

They surrounded us. Before I could think about how to get out of it, Moochie made a loud Kung Fu scream, jumped into the air, flipped on his hands, and like an expert kicked two of the guys in the face. They plopped out-cold on the ground, leaving only the big guy. Moochie moved his hands and shifted into a fighting stance like Bruce Lee, making Chinese noises. *"Aiiiiiiiiiiiiie!"*

The big guy got scared and ran off.

"Damn, Moochie, I didn't know you could fight like that."

"I didn't know you couldn't," he said.

I spent several nights on my research paper, writing page after page, reading articles and books on TV, and thinking of my own life with TV. When Sally got home from work she would watch me for a while, yawn, and then she would go to bed while I continued working.

When I had been living with my parents in Fremont, all I did when I was home was watch TV, anything from Perry Mason reruns to network sitcoms. When I wasn't watching TV, I was hanging out with friends (I had friends in Fremont), getting high, wasting my time doing nothing. I got all F's my first year of high school. The principal threatened to send me to continuation. Then I got caught selling joints in the bathroom.

Not only did he kick me out of school, but he had me arrested, too. The cops also sent about a dozen officers to my house to search my room. They found about a hundred tabs of LSD, two ounces of marijuana, and a little bit of cocaine. They threatened my parents with arrest, questioning how they couldn't know I had such a cache of drugs. After I got out of the Hall, my father wanted to kill me. He picked me up by my collar and pushed me hard against the wall, his face inches from mine. "You're a worthless piece of shit," he said. My mom suggested I go and live with my sister.

Here we had no TV except the black and white that only got two channels, so it was rarely on. I was glad because that encouraged me to write and study. With Sally working nights, I was always alone, and that helped too. What else was there to do?

I included in my essay not only the surveys and the research, but personal experience. By the time I was done with the paper, it had twelve typed pages. Mr. Benard must have read it the first night. The next day he raved about me in front of the class, saying that I was bound for success. Andy seemed to be squirming in the back.

The student teacher from the university never showed up. When the questionnaires and some grammar exercises from a textbook were due, Mr. Benard needed help because the students wanted to know if they had done them right. They needed individual clarification on things they didn't understand. He asked me if I wouldn't mind helping some of them.

My half of the Mexican table became a place where I tutored these white students. I helped them with grammar, spelling, and, most importantly, to understand the ideas they encountered in their readings. After a while, most of the students preferred coming to me over Mr. Benard. I would compliment their work in language they could understand. One girl wanted me to explain what was theme, and the conversation (I used movies as examples of how to identify theme) got so involved that after the bell rang we walked out together to the smoking section, lit up, and continued talking. At some point, she realized she was with someone who wasn't cool, so she left and talked to me only in class.

One day during class, in a break from tutoring, Pilar looked up from her paper at me. She just stared, like I had done something wrong.

"What?" I said.

"You never write no more."

"Sure, I do, just not in class."

"Well, since you don't have no more time for me, I brought you something."

"What?" I asked.

"I bring you lunch."

She showed me a brown paper bag heavy with home and let me smell it.

"Wow, that smells great. What is it?"

"*Real* Mexican food," she said. "Not Taco Bell."

At lunch we sat on a bench in the quad and ate our tacos. Pilar looked at me for a reaction, but I didn't want to compliment her on her cooking. I wanted to compliment her on her writing.

"What's going to be your major in college?" I asked her.

"I'm not going to college," she said.

"Why not?" I asked.

"I am getting married."

"Oh, yeah? What if no one wants to marry you?"

"I am engaged already," she said.

"Really?"

"We get married in one year. He is in Mexico."

She took a small bite from her taco. I felt sorry for her, not because marriage was bad, but because I feared what would become of her. I had no right to feel that way, but I couldn't help but picture her surrounded by a bunch of kids before she had a chance to discover who she was, like I was beginning to discover about myself. But maybe she already knew who she was.

"He won't get jealous, will he?" I asked. "That you're eating with me. You know, another man?"

She giggled. "You? No. You? You're like my cousin. My American cousin."

For midterms the students had to have their assignments checked and approved, and the only two people who could do that were me and Benard. One day we were busy most of the period, but then it died down, and Mr. Benard, from his desk, looked over at me and smiled. Then we heard footsteps and we both turned around. It was Andy, carrying his assignment to the front of the class. It wasn't clear which one of us he would approach. Andy stopped and looked at us, as if he, too, didn't know. Finally, he chose Mr. Benard, who took his work, looked at it, and shook his head as if he thought Andy was the biggest idiot in the world.

A little later, a student from the back of the class asked what it meant to be "a fly on the wall," an easy enough concept that Mr. Benard complicated by using words like "objectivity" and "neutrality." When he saw that the class didn't understand, he asked me to try. I stood up, put my hands in my pockets, and strolled to the front of the table.

"Let's say you have some really good bud," I said. "Green sticky bud, the kind that smells like a skunk when you open the bag."

The stoners laughed, and some of them looked at Benard wondering if he was going to let me continue.

"I'm not talking that cheap rag weed, fifty cents a joint stuff that makes your eyes red and heavy, that makes you so damn sleepy all you can do is say, 'Duh, I'm stoned.'"

They laughed.

"I'm talking the best. You take a few hits. It's different. If you're in class for example, it's like you're not really in class. It's like your watching it on TV only it's not TV either. It's real. You're there, but you're not a part of the scene. You're like a fly on the wall. Just watching. And because you don't belong to the action taking place, you're able to see things clearer than those who are."

One day in class Mr. Benard asked me to keep order while he went to the office. Immediately after he left, Andy got up and started walking around giving everyone a hard time. Strangely enough, people told him to knock it off because they were reading. But he wouldn't stop. He started throwing wads of paper across the room.

"Andy?" I finally said from my table.

"What? You got a problem?" he said, walking toward me.

"*I* don't have the problem," I said, standing up.

"You do now," he said.

Suddenly a girl from the back of the class, the one to whom I had explained theme, said, "Leave him alone, Andy. He's cool."

"Yeah," said another guy. "He's hell of a lot cooler than Benard."

Andy mumbled something and sat back down. After that he was quiet. He read his book and he was quiet.

"Hey, Guerra!" I heard Andy yell as I walked out of the smoking section one afternoon. I pretended not to hear him and continued walking toward the volleyball games. I knew this was it. Sweat dripped down my back. Spots of moisture grew like moons beneath my armpits. Students with colorful clothes and tanned skin blurred by my vision as I tried to stay focused on my destination, the volleyball game, where the Chicanos were slaughtering white guys with white tennis shoes and white teeth.

"Hey, Guerra," he yelled again. "I want to show you something."

The swimming pool across the campus sparkled in the sun. The ball thumped and flew. He was right behind me.

He said, "If you don't stop, I'm going to kick some ass."

I stopped.

I turned around.

His cheeks looked so fat under his glasses that I imagined grabbing them within my fists and pulling his face toward my rising knee, smashing his glasses on impact, blood flowing from his eyes, all over my pant leg, soaking my jeans; and all other eyes in school would be on me, a man who couldn't take it any more. A crazy man.

The Chicanos would ask me to join their volleyball team.

"I got something to show you, Guerra."

He took a folded paper out of his back pocket. Suddenly he looked embarrassed. He unfolded it and held it out to me.

"Can you look at my history paper?" he asked.

He was a helpless lion with a thorn in his paw. His big eyelashes swept up and down over his blue eyes, and he said, "I mean, maybe you can help me with my errors. I don't write too good."

While we were outside watching the world go by, Moochie asked me what it was to be an American. He had to go back to Mongolia that afternoon, and he really wanted to know. I looked down the street at my neighborhood without sidewalks, with shabby homes and broken down cars on the curb, and I thought about it.

"Come here," I said. "I'm going to show you America."

He followed me into the apartment, through the living room, down the dark hallway where I stopped. Still walking, he bumped into me.

"What are we doing in the dark?" he asked.

"I'm showing you America."

I flicked on the lights. Against the wall at the end of the

hall was a full-length mirror. I looked at Moochie in that mirror. I looked at myself too. Then he looked in the mirror. He
put his arm around me and smiled as if he were posing for a
picture.

"There you go," I said. "That's America."

I got straight A's that semester which was enough for my mom to
convince my dad that I was ready to go back to Fremont. I resisted,
but only a little because I wanted to find out if I could be successful
there, too. So I went. When I was registering for high school, I signed
up for Advanced Composition. The counselor called me in and
informed me that I couldn't take it.

"Why?" I asked. "English is my best subject."

"According to your records, you only had remedial English. Basic
Reading. I'm afraid this composition course is too advanced for you."

I told him about Benard's class, about the Intermediate Comp, the
tutoring of students, and the Mexican table. He looked me up and
down as if sizing me up. Then he stood.

"I'm sorry, all we have to go by are your transcripts."

Although I should have been angry at Mr. Benard, I wasn't. I
walked out of the counselor's office onto the polished floor of the
main office. I stood for a while watching the students outside walk to
class. This was all right. I walked into the sunlight.

Spring Break

Cipri said he knew where we could get a cow. He said that out in the hills, about twenty miles from the city, we could find a bunch of them, totally unsupervised by the wealthy farmer he used to work for. He was excited, almost jumping up and down. "I tell you, I've worked for that asshole long enough to know that the cows are left on their own on Sundays. I was the only one who ever drove out there on weekends. I know he ain't replaced me yet." He was standing between the couch, where Domingo lay wrapped to his neck in a baby-blue comforter, and the sliding glass door to the balcony, where I sat on a short-legged lawn chair. Far beyond the even row of apartment rooftops with white rocks and air conditioners, I could see gray patches of pine and eucalyptus trees, and then beyond that, the brown foothills miles outside of town. I could barely see the purple mountains, so vague they faded in and out of the clouds and sky.

"Would you pay attention?" he said to me. He wore baggy gray pants and an untucked pullover shirt. The acne on his face ("crater face," we used to call him) and his big round cheeks and large white teeth made him look sort of cartoonish, like he was always smiling, like the kid on the cover of *Mad Magazine* or a Chicano Milton Berle.

"We'll take it to Earlimart," he said to me. "Butcher it in mom's backyard."

"I think you're crazy, Cipri," said Domingo, who reached for a Pepsi can he had sitting on the coffee table. The comforter slipped off him, all the way to his briefs, his body pale and skinny like an old man. "I'm not going to jail over a cow," he said, sipping his Pepsi.

"You guys are really sad," Cipri said. "Domingo, you know damn well it's a great idea. A hell of a lot better than that shit you do. You know what he does? He orders a great big lunch at the cafeteria at school, and then he walks by the cashier pretending like he's getting the condiments—you know, ketchup and shit?—then he keeps on walking without paying. Domingo's going to get thrown out of school and shit. I'm telling him."

"They can't catch me. All I got to say is I was going to put ketchup on my food. What can they say? Besides, I pay a lot of money for tuition. It's not like I'm stealing from the poor."

"Yeah, and my ex-fucking boss ain't going to miss one cow. He's got hundreds—thousands—of those bastards."

I stood up from the lawn chair and was about to go back across the threshold when I noticed an apartment door opening. It was the young Chilean woman who lived at ground level a few buildings down. I had been staying at my brother Cipri's apartment near Fresno State University all week, and had seen her several times, even had small talk with her at the mailboxes one day. She was an international student with two years left before she could go back home. Her building was connected to Cipri's by an asphalt path lined on both sides by small trees that at the beginning of spring bloomed white flowers with a pungent smell, like wet laundry. Cipri and Domingo weren't used to me staying there and leaving the sliding glass door open all the time, and they complained about the smell the entire week that I was with them. The Chilean student stepped out her door, swinging a red back-pack over her shoulder.

"What if we get caught?" asked Domingo.

I heard Domingo say something, and then Cipri got worked up into a speech, as if he were trying to motivate soldiers on their way to the front. White petals fell from the treetops and floated down like butterflies in the sunlight, into her long black hair, up against her body, and then onto the dark path. I wondered how she felt so far away from home, if she got lonely and depressed. I breathed in the odor of the flowers and realized that I really liked that smell. It was a terrible smell, but I liked it. I wondered what the trees smelled like where she was from. I wanted to say something to her as she passed, perhaps only a hello. Perhaps I would tell her, "I know, I know, how you feel."

Cipri was talking louder, cussing every other word, and Domingo was trying to argue with him. When she passed directly beneath the balcony, I looked down, smiled largely, and said "Hello," waving my arm. And at that same moment Cipri yelled—loud enough for the entire complex to hear—"Don't be such a pussy!"

The student bent her head and quickened her walk.

"Can you imagine all the fucking meat we'd get? We'll have a big feast. Why shouldn't we take one of his cows? The *gabacho*'s rich. We're poor and shit. People like us got to do this kind of shit just to survive."

"You could have gone to school, too, Cipri," I said.

"What the fuck does that got to do with it? Domingo's going to school and he's still poor. Shit, his mom can't even afford to call him on the phone. And whenever he makes any money himself, he sends it to her. Not everybody's a Harvard boy and shit—we don't have everyone paying our way and shit. I mean, I'm proud of you, you know that. But not everyone's like you. And fuck, you're over there in fucking Massachusetts and shit. That's where those—what's his name, man?—the Kennedys and shit. That's where they're from. Over there, being poor is an idea in a book. And there ain't no Chicanos there neither. I mean, if there are, they're like you. Every time you go back to Earlimart, you don't even know how to talk to people no more."

"I get along fine with everyone," I said. I was getting angry.

"No, you don't. Everyone thinks you think you're too good and shit. But I know that's not it. I know it's because you got so much education over there that you don't know how to talk to us like you used to. We're like theories to you and shit. You don't even know what it's like. Come on, Choco, let's have a party tonight. We'll invite all of Earlimart, the whole town—anybody who wants to eat—even the fucking *mojados*. What harm is there in stealing one cow from a rich fucker that ain't going to notice anyway?"

"Hey, Cipri, you think we could make those tri-tip things. You know, like we had at that barbecue?" Domingo was reaching down for his can of Pepsi.

"Shit yeah. Anything we want. Just talk to him." He pointed to me.

"Come on," Domingo said. "Those tri-tips are good!"

The weather was nice, so we had the windows of Cipri's truck rolled down. Cool air flooded the cab, our hair and clothes snapping like whips, the sound drowning out the murmur of the stereo. From up close, the foothills glared bright green, and there were orange trees on both sides of the highway, so leafy that they looked like rows of giant green bushes—the dark trails of dirt between them shuffling by our vision like a deck of cards. Domingo sat in the middle, the gearshift between his knees and his eyes closed and face scrunched up as if he couldn't be any more uncomfortable. Domingo had been our best friend for years. We considered him our cousin. Now he was rooming with Cipri while working on a degree in Criminology at Fresno State. His family lived down the street from ours, in Earlimart, a small farm-working community near Delano, made up almost entirely of Mexicans. Domingo's family came from the hills of Durango, from a small village without electricity or direct communication with the rest of the world. Part of the journey there included a six-hour ride on a mule, and during picking season, about fifty of his relatives, an entire village, came to Earlimart, to our street, and they would stay until the picking was over. Our street was called "Wetback Row" by the second- and third-generation Chicanos, who didn't always get along with the migrants. At the peak of the season, our street was alive on weekend nights as hundreds of people, mostly men, drank and barbe-cued, walked up and down the street, and laughed and screamed. Though Cipri and I were second generation, we lived on Wetback Row and got along fine with everyone. It was our home.

Now Cipri was telling us why the guy who owned the cows had fired him.

"I says, 'I don't get paid to tell those Mexicans what to do. I'm a poor son of a bitch just like them. If you wanna tell them to do shit, you got to do it.' I mean, he thinks I'm going to go up to these *campesinos*—and I swear the oldest one looks just like grandpa, man. I mean, I almost wanna kiss the *viejo* every time I see him. My boss wants me to tell them what to do and then to fire one of them and shit."

"Maybe you could go back to school," I said, sounding trite and insincere.

"Back? What do you mean *back?*"

"I have to go to the bathroom," said Domingo, his eyes still closed. We both just looked at him as if we forgot that he was between us.

"Domingo has to go to the little boy's room," I said.

"Domingo's going to have to get yellow-eyed."

The road passed through the rock and earth of the verdant foothills, looking as if it were freshly cut, and ahead of us we could see the dark purple, pine-topped mountains. The road went up and over a hill beyond which appeared a series of smaller hills, all covered with what looked like evenly cut lawn. A bunch of cows and steers were scattered around eating grass and looking dumbly into the air. There was so much of it, so many hills with cattle, that it seemed to go on and on—some of the cattle merely brown and black dots on the green horizon. The white wooden fences swirled along the highway, looking as if the boards were made of rubber.

"This is it," said Cipri.

On my side of the street there was a narrow dirt road. Cipri slowed the truck down and turned onto the dirt road. We approached the metal gate and Cipri got out. He unlocked it with his key, swung it open, and got back in. The cows didn't even seem to notice us as we drove between them. Cipri stopped the truck abruptly, causing Domingo to jerk forward. "Let's go get us a cow, gentlemen." He stepped out and slammed the door behind him, walked over to the gate, and closed it. I looked at Domingo, and then I opened the door and got out and left it open for him. The sun was halfway behind a foothill, tar and rocks sparkling like diamonds on the highway. The double lines down the middle shined like strips of silver.

A cool breeze carried the smell of cow dung. "Let's hurry up," I said. "It smells."

Cipri took in a huge breath and said, "Ah, wilderness!"

"Which one do we want?" said Domingo.

"That one," he said, pointing at the cow nearest us, a dumb-looking bovine watching us with indifferent, big, brown eyes, and chewing slowly a mouth full of grass.

"No, not that one," I said.

"Why the hell not?" asked Cipri.

"Well . . ." I was unsure how to explain it.

"He's cute," said Domingo.

"All right, fine," I said. "I guess one cow's just as good as another. How are we going to get him into the truck?"

"We got to kill him first." Cipri walked back to the truck, opened the door, and lifted the seat forward, pulling out a wooden baseball bat.

"You can't kill a cow with a baseball bat," I objected.

"That. And this," he said, pulling out a pocket knife.

"You can't kill him with those."

"Watch me." Cipri walked over to the cow. He held the bat over his head like John Henry about to pound his sledge hammer and brought it down on the head of the cow, who jerked in pain, shook his ears and ran away.

"You don't know anything about cows, do you? You don't know a thing." I had expected he did.

"I know they make great steak dinners and shit. I told you I only used to come out here once a week. I spent all my time at the store. But all I got to do is hit one of them in the right spot. That's all." He scanned the hillside until he found the one he wanted to kill. "I'll try that one." He walked over to a huge steer who had his muscled neck down, and who was chomping grass. "The secret is in the grip." Like a batter he planted his feet in the moist ground, assumed the batter's position, and tested the weight of the bat by swinging it back and forth a few times. Then he pulled it back as he ran up to the steer and swung full force onto the head. The animal shook off the pain, twitched his ears and then charged Cipri, who jumped aside smoothly, shifting his weight, letting the animal brush against him, then he whacked it on the head again. He was yelling "Olé" as he chased the steer and batted it on the back, daring it to charge him. The steer hopped away like a gazelle.

"Maybe you should have brought a gun." Again we forgot he was with us, so when Domingo said this, we both jumped. I was sure that Cipri, like me, had started to feel guilty about being so cruel to innocent animals, and that he thought, for a split moment, that one of the cows had said something. I realized, though, that Cipri thought it was the voice of the owner, not a cow. Cipri felt the fear of being caught.

But the voice was only Domingo's. He looked back and forth at us with his own big, brown eyes.

"What the hell are you talking about?" Cipri was quite irritated.

"Well it's not doing the job, is it?"

"Just shut up, Domingo, man. You got nothing important to say."

"Both of you guys shut up and give me the knife and the bat," I said. "I'll kill it." I wanted to get it over with.

Cipri held the bat possessively. "I'll do it," he said. "One more cow," he whispered, walking determinedly up the hill toward a cluster of them. When he got about twenty feet way from them, he ran up the hill with the bat over his head. The cows started to run in all directions while Cipri swung the bat around like a primal club. He thumped a few heads and whacked a few backs, causing cows to dart off even more frantically, scattering across the hill. Some charged at him, but Cipri twisted and jumped, batting them as they went by and yelling, "DIIIE!" But none of them were dying; they were just scared and running.

"DIIIE!"

And something clicked inside me.

"Cipri, you ain't doing shit to them fuckers," I screamed.

Domingo looked at me like I was the crazy one, not Cipri, who was running after cows and batting them, going now for quantity, and getting quite a few.

"Cipri," I yelled. "You ain't doing shit but jacking off. We're here to get some fucking meat, remember?"

Cipri stopped on the top of the hill holding the bat by his side, breathing hard and smiling. "This is great!"

He started to walk down the hill and I met him halfway up, grabbed the bat and asked him for the knife, which he pulled out of his pants pocket and handed to me. Then, without yelling or saying a word, just sort of growling, I ran up the hill toward a small, white steer. He wasn't sure which way to run away from me, so he just stood there dumbfounded. I threw down the baseball bat, pulled the blade out of the knife, and ran toward the beast. The knife was bigger than I expected, and I grasped the black handle firmly in my fist. When I reached him, he decided to turn around, so I jumped on him, grabbed his ear with my free hand, and stuck the knife with all my strength into his head. He jerked and tried to shake off the pain, and tried to charge at me, his powerful neck pushing up, but I was too quick with the knife for him to fight for very long. I twisted the knife around and pulled it out, then stuck it in again and twisted it again. I grabbed onto his head, letting it move me from side to side until I could feel his hot blood pour over my arms. His strength died away quicker than I expected. I expected a longer fight, but he suddenly quit. He just stood there letting me do it. I stabbed him over and over and poked out both of his eyes. I felt my own wet tears dripping on my arm, and the murmur I heard was me crying like a little kid, stabbing over and over. I ran for the bat, picked it up, and went back to the bloody-headed steer and started pounding him over the head, and, finally, he fell. But I still whacked him some more until Cipri and Domingo ran up the hill, Cipri yelling, "Son of a bitch. Homeboy's tough."

When they got to where I was thumping the steer with the bat, I stopped. I put the bat down, wiped the sweat from my forehead and the tears from my raw cheeks. "Damn," I muttered.

"Let's get this puppy loaded," Cipri said. He ran to the truck and backed it up against the hill. He opened the tailgate so it was about even with the hill, and we pushed and pulled the steer until we could slide it into the back.

It was dark when we pulled up to mom's, a small, white, wooden house with a large front yard and a dirt driveway to the side. A carport sagged over her '63 Plymouth on blocks. Beyond that was the huge backyard, which was one part lawn, one part cement patio with splintered picnic benches underneath an aluminum canopy, and one part dry dirt and junk. A clear night, the moon looked like a swimming pool glowing coolly in the dark, purple sky. The tall trees around the backyard, in front of and behind the six-foot fence, made it seem like we were secluded from everyone else, secured behind walls. We all felt a sense of pride as we unloaded the animal from the back of the truck and laid him on the dirt. The steer's face looked like it had been pecked by birds. We stood around admiring it. All the lights were off in mom's house, which meant she was still at my sister's, where she stayed on Sundays so she wouldn't have to be alone.

"What are you going to butcher it with?" asked Domingo.

I looked at Cipri for a response, but he just looked down at the cow, his big eyes reflecting the moon.

"What are you going to use to butcher the cow?" I asked him.

"Hell, I don't know. Knives and shit," he said.

"You better know how to butcher it," I said.

"We just take the meat, man," he said to me, not really under-standing my concern. "We'll get some good steaks. Filets and shit."

"How do you think we're supposed to get the meat? You think it's going to come out of the cow when we order it? You have to butcher it."

"We'll just cut it out," he said.

"Show me," I said, handing him the knife.

He pulled the blade out and bent down over the steer. Sticking the knife in the steer's side, he tried to cut across, but it was too difficult.

"You have to cut the head off first, Cipri," said Domingo.

"I don't got to do shit," said Cipri, pulling the knife out of the steer and sticking it back in. He tried for about five minutes, and finally he put the knife down and took a deep breath. "I need a bigger knife."

Of course, he didn't know what he was doing, and after trying for about an hour with knives, axes, a crowbar, and any other tool that looked like it might be useful, he gave up. The steer looked like a *chu-pacabra* victim.

We sat quietly in the dark in my mom's backyard. Domingo was on a bench under the aluminum canopy. I was seated with my back against the wooden fence. I didn't care when I felt a bug crawl up my back. Cipri stood over his mess, looking down on it. He seemed to be smiling, but he wasn't. That was just the shape of his face. It started to get chilly, and Domingo looked like he wanted to go back to the apart-ment. So did I. I would be leaving in two days to go back to school, so I wanted to spend one more night at Cipri's place. When I got back to Fresno, I would take a long walk on campus and watch the students study in the library or the student lounge. I would look for the Chilean student and start up a conversation with her. I would tell her that after I graduate, I may go back to Earlimart and teach at the high school in Delano, or I may decide to go to law school like I had originally intended, but that I didn't care one way or the other what I did, as long as I was near my home. I hated Harvard. I hated the East Coast.

But before that could happen, Domingo grabbed a shovel from against the house and started digging a hole in the middle of the yard. Dirt flew in the air, sparkling in the moonlight, landing and forming a fresh pile.

I rose up from the soil.

I grabbed a pick, then I joined Domingo, cracking the earthy chunks, loosening it so he could more easily shovel the dirt. Cipri joined with another shovel, and we spent about two hours shoveling and picking, wiping sweat and dirt from our faces, not saying much at all, just digging until we had a hole big enough to bury it in.

Torture Fantasy

Oz Garcia, a U.S. Postal clerk, slammed hard against the brick floor. He landed fingers and knees first and hurt so badly he screamed. The relentless pounding on the door was followed by a booming voice, "Garcia? Oz Garcia?" and then the doorbell rang seven times and then seven more.

"Hold it! Hold it!" Oz yelled.

"Open up!" demanded the voice.

Boom Boom Boom

"I'm fricken coming," said Oz.

As he pulled it open, he yelled, "What the hell do you"—but now seeing who it was, he finished his sentence a lot softer than he began it, almost a squeak now—"want?"

There were four of them.

"Yes?" he offered.

They stood erect, dressed in military uniforms, four young men with blonde hair and blue eyes. The one in the middle was barely a man, maybe seventeen, but he was tall and muscular, his uniform stretching. His face was red firm and handsome and wide and his features cut well like an American Movie Hero. He had short hair sticking straight up. His nose shined. His chest heaved with air, "Oz Garcia?"

Oz felt pain in his fingers as he nervously rubbed them. The young soldier's fingers were thick as chorizo, his hand the width of a flour tortilla. The other men looked straight ahead at attention. Oz let go of his fingers. "I'm he," he answered.

"Come with us," shouted the young man. "You have five minutes to gather your things."

"But who are you?"

"The timer has started, Garcia. Five minutes."

Trying to sound formal and professional, Oz asked, "To what does this pertain?"

His neighbor Jobby, peering from behind the blue curtains next door, moved away from the window when Oz looked over.

"This is a joke from Jobby, right? Well, tell him it was a good one." Oz laughed. "Whew! You boys are very convincing. Thank you, and bye."

He tried to close the door but in unison the men produced handguns.

"Hey, who are you guys?"

They marched seven steps forward, backing Oz into his house. He tripped on the steps and fell.

"You have three minutes now to get your things or we take you as is."

"Where exactly is it you are 'taking' me?" he asked, quoting "taking" with his fingers. He stood up, but they didn't answer. "Well, then I guess I better get some things together. Ha, ha. I'll get them right now, gentlemen, so we can go. Three minutes, right? Let's see." He looked around his living room. "There anything here I want to take? I tell you what, if I knew where we were going I could have a better idea about what to take. But I guess you boys ain't allowed to divulge that information. No, sir. You boys are pretty low on the pecking order, I imagine. So, we're going for, how long? The afternoon?"

The men were silent and stiff.

The living room had windows on all sides and sun lit up the place. The insignias on their uniforms shone. Oz moved in to get a closer look. Their badges said, "B. Flaco," an image of a lighthouse and moon.

"Two minutes," announced the young man, still staring straight ahead as if at attention.

"Two? Okay," he looked around. He didn't want to take the couch, of course, that would be silly. He giggled when he thought of himself saying to the boys, "Can you help me with this," as he bent over to grab one end.

He didn't need to take the brightly colored Mexican blanket draped over the couch.

He didn't want to take his portable stereo since all that worked was the radio, and they never played songs he liked except for Sunday afternoons from three to five on the public broadcasting station. The old TV with rabbit ear antennae and dials you had to turn with your hand like an oven sat lopsided on a cardboard box. His parka. Hanging over the bright yellow chair facing the window. Yes, he would take his parka. He removed it from the chair and said to the boys, "Can I get stuff from my bedroom?"

Still and stiff as statues, they didn't answer.

"Okay then. I'll be right back."

In his room he looked around, the clothes on the floor, the blankets and sheets strewn down the side of the bed, the colognes and aftershave on the dresser with the mirror where he caught a glimpse of himself. Dark, flabby face, baby black eyes, double chin with stubble.

He tried to concentrate on what to take: Perhaps his turtle Morgan, who lay on his back on the bed, eyes of beads staring up and sewed-on smile.

The men marched into the bedroom. "Time's up."

Oz grabbed a pillow. With a pillow in one arm and the parka in the other, they led him to the door, and as they were opening it, he turned around to take one last look. At the end of the narrow living room, the yellow chair, facing outward at the wood-framed window, soaked in the sunlight.

They led him onto a path lined by bushes with little red berries that looked like dangling gumballs. The compound had barracks with sheet metal roofs and a tower with a guard carrying a rifle and surveying the landscape with oversized binoculars that made his eyes look gigantic. There were tall trees all around. A sign on a wooden stake that read "registration" pointed them into double automatic doors, on which the logo was affixed, "B. Flaco," the lighthouse and the moon. They led him inside where speakers hanging from the four corners of the ceiling played the Muzak grocery store instrumental version of "I Got You Babe" by Sonny and Cher. The boys left him standing there and they disappeared. Other than the Muzak the place was quiet.

And still.

So still that Oz could hear everything, the sound of his feet shifting; his breathing hard because he was out of breath from the walk; a pencil tapping "Shave and a Haircut" at the front desk, where a bald-headed man was on the telephone saying, uh uh uhm. A water cooler gurgled in another room. The man put the phone on the receiver and looked up. "Oz! Good to see you, fella."

"Marvin!" said Oz.

"How you doing, fella?" Marvin asked, standing up. He was about a foot shorter than Oz. His eyes were so close together they almost looked attached to each other. "Welcome," Marvin said, holding out his arms and smiling. Then the smile gave way to a frown and his arms slowly came down. "Well, I guess 'welcome' may not be the appropriate greeting for this situation."

"I would think not," said Oz, shaking his head. "Welcome? No, not *welcome. Blitzkrieg* maybe. Maybe that's what you should say." Oz put his hands on his hips. He was shaped like an egg. "You should say *blitzkrieg*. That's what you should say. It would sure be more sufficient than—what was it?—'welcome.' Much more, Marvin."

"You're right, Oz. From now on that's what I'll say. Next time someone new walks into that door I'll say, 'Blitzkrieg!'"

Hell.

Pure hell.

They let him sleep only four hours before they violently pulled him from his cot each cold, dark morning and pushed him into the exercise yard where, in a patch of dirt and gravel surrounded by tall chain link fences with barbed wire around the top and brightly lit by search lights which stung his eyes, they made him start with two hundred jumping jacks. He tired excessively after the first ten and was ready to stop after fifty, but he was better off dealing with the pain, because whenever he put his arms down—even for a flash—they added one hundred more. He thought about just giving up, but the very same young man who had come to his door, prodded him with a steel stick every time he stopped. "One hundred more, Garcia," he'd say.

The first seven mornings it took over an hour to complete the jumping jacks. After the jumping jacks came the ten-mile run—with his arms full of logs and a heavy backpack on his shoulders—over hills and fallen trees and through meadows and murky creeks that smelled of sewage. And whenever he stopped running or dropped a log, there was that boy running behind to prod him on the side with the steel stick. The first several times Oz couldn't breath after the first hundred yards, but no amount of crying or pleading would convince them to take it easy on him.

After the run he was given breakfast, juice, water, and butterless toast. The one time he asked for butter—"please, just a tiny tab, or else, if you will, some marmalade, perhaps orange"—they took away his food and he went hungry all day, barely able to stand up during weight training. For lunch he was served beans and rice without flavor, and for dinner: bread and steamed grey vegetables and an apple for dessert, his favorite part of the day. While the soldiers watched, perhaps to make sure he hadn't somehow stuffed in his pocket a carnita burrito, he slowly ate the apple, wanting that part of his day to last the longest. By the time he got to his cabin at the end of each day, he was too tired to even watch TV, especially since the set they provided him was powered by a treadmill and was like running uphill.

One bright day, during his run, when the soldier was distracted by a squawking crow that dived at his head like a mad bird, Oz sneaked away on his run and found the bushes with the little red berries dangling like gumdrops. He picked one, held it in his plump fingers and examined it closely. It looked edible.

As if he were a giant trying to eat an apple, he took a tiny bite. He chewed. It tasted bittersweet. He popped the rest of it into his mouth and furiously picked the berries and shoved them into his cheeks, which got full and fat, and he made yum yum sounds and breathed through his nose until his stomach began to fill. He heard branches snap, and he looked up. Two soldiers dragged him away. "Where are you taking me?" he cried. "You have to understand. I'm not used to this."

They dragged him to a wooden shack at the foot of the guard tower. The creaky wooden door opened onto an empty room which was hot and dim. Sun slipped through the slats of wood that made up the wall, imposing stripes on the floor, in the middle of which lay a door that looked as if it had fallen, but it was an entrance into a sub-terranean room with no steps down. The soldiers threw Oz in. He had to get on his knees and bend over before they could close him into the wet darkness. He heard the lock click shut. He was scrunched. Packed in.

The eyes of creatures and monsters lit up, and across from where he was hunched over, a set of shiny sharp teeth, like those of a Cheshire cat about to attack a cornered mouse, smiled at him. He yelled and screamed and pounded on the door, but the guards were gone. Oz cried and mumbled, "Please no. Please no." He wanted to— was ready to—accept the inevitability of death. He lay on the moist earth, wiped off something wet crawling across his face, and closed his eyes.

But he didn't die.

He tingled and itched all over. As he scratched, he could feel the welts that had broken out all over his body and imagined what he looked like. Like Jobby's face, all that red and purple acne. This made him laugh. And when he opened his eyes, he saw a tiny dot of light at the end of what seemed to be a long tunnel. He crawled through it, barely able to fit, until he reached the other side. A wood and rope bridge swayed over a thick green creek, so cold he could feel it on his body as he crossed into a forest, which was green and prosperous, with fruits of all sizes, shapes, and colors, some dripping with sweetness and buzzing with happy bees. Inside of a three-sided hut made of rustic wood, an ancient Mexican lady in the shadows was hunched over a red hot comal, patting the tortilla dough in her hands as she sang an old Christian lullaby. "We have no money here," he heard himself say. Her laughter echoed through the forest.

Her hand reached out toward him, becoming huge and blocking his view, the skin wrinkled, oily like a snake, holding a fat steaming tortilla with a melting slab of butter on top. "One for free," she said.

Oz gobbled it up but spit it out because it tasted like mud.

"Get it?" the lady laughed. "Get it?"

At the bank of the river, a naked indigenous girl was catching fish with her hands, laughing like a child as she sloshed around the cool, blue water, which sparkled at her finger tips like magic dust. The fish jumping out of her grasp smiled and giggled and wagged their tail fins as if they were playing tag. Over the trees that surrounded the forest hung the sun, which turned into a sliver of moon as darkness began to descend and then back to sun as light came back. The naked girl, dripping wet, her long black hair plastered against her smooth shoulder, looked at Oz and coyly smiled.

An Aztec warrior, muscular and young, dressed in loincloth and plumed headdress, appeared between two trees. He looked like the painting of the Aztec with the dead girl in his arms, sans the girl. He pointed his battle ax at Oz. Then he came running after him. His teeth were clenched in anger, the muscles on his arms and chest palpitating. Oz ran as fast as he could, the forest blurring by him, the fruit, the bushes, a Chinese guy playing a sad cello.

He quit running, although the cello continued to echo like a voice in mourning, when he came upon a small white room, narrow and empty except for a chair at the end, his yellow chair facing a window.

He wanted to turn away but everywhere he faced the chair was there. He wished someone was sitting in the chair, like Jobby, looking off into a meadow where seven peach trees blossoming with lavender flowers were swaying.

Then it happened. Wearing his overalls, Jobby sat at the chair watching seven peach trees blossoming with lavender flowers.

"What you looking at?" Oz asked.

"Sssh!" Jobby indicated with a finger over his thin, dry lips. "Listen."

All he heard was the cello.

"So sad," said Jobby.

Oz laughed, because he pictured a piano falling from the sky and squashing Jobby, and then it did: a piano dropped from the sky and squashed Jobby, dust flying out from the sides. The cello stopped. Once the piano settled, it began to rock and shake and then tumbled over, and Jobby emerged with a big knot on his head. "Ow, that smarts," he said.

Oz laughed.

One time, when he had been between sleep and nonsleep, he began to have dreams, images really, shards of dreams, and he found because he was still awake that he could put the pieces together to create the dream he had wanted. He tried that with the jungle. "You know what I'd like to see?" he said to himself.

"Art."

And sure enough, beyond a thicket rich with those little red berries that looked like gumdrops, art hung from the tree trunks, the *Mona Lisa*, *Starry Night*, *The Last Supper*.

"I want my turtle Morgan to be the art dealer," he said, and there, sitting on a chair, eyes of beads staring off because they were fixed, sat Morgan, with his happy thread smile.

Anything he wanted he willed and it happened, so when the soldiers came for him later on, days later perhaps, who knew?—he was having a good time. The sun shot into the hole and the forest disappeared into white noise. Oz looked up.

"Come on, just a little while longer," he said.

After that day Oz had no problem with the regimen. The jumping jacks he did in no time, and he began to enjoy the ten-mile run, watching the sun rise like a neon coin over the piggy back of the distant mountains, the leaves filled with twittering light, the birds happily singing the beauty of the day. Yet he ran so fast that the boy had trouble keeping up. He added more weights to his exercise and ate, measurably and slowly, what they put before him. At night, he would sometimes get on the treadmill and watch *Seinfeld,* his favorite sitcom, laughing aloud as he trudged on.

Oz became a solid and healthy man. When he returned to his job at the post office and people got impatient because the line was long or because they were in a hurry, he would stamp the letters with such force that his counter shook. He'd peer right at the offender, who would smile humbly and quietly step back in line. When it was their turn, they greeted Oz by saying, "Hello, sir. Lovely day, isn't it?"

Slow and Good

O range and white cat sleeping on the sidewalk sees us coming and darts across a lawn. Shadows of trees are spirits. The trunks are black. Over rooftops and fences, a half moon glows above the foothills, shadows of jagged, rising earth. Our footsteps echo on the sidewalk, Johnny de la Rosa, Gilbert Sanchez, and me. David Romero isn't with us because his parents don't let him out at night, but we feel his presence, his slicked-back black hair like a vampire and those crooked front teeth. Some kids coming from the opposite direction, their laughter fading in and out of air, see us and they're silent. They cross the street, three silhouettes that are small and skinny. Old people peer at us from behind curtains. A police car slows down, the dash light shining on the cop's chest and badge as he watches us. Gilbert pounds his own chest with a fist, a loud thump. His eyeglasses rattle. "We'll get him too," he says. We keep walking. Determined. We're on a mission.

We walk through the P Street underpass, a cement hallway lit by street lamps protected in cages. The headlights of cars project our shadows weirdly against the concrete walls. We reach the full bowling alley parking lot and I break antennas off the cars as I pass. Snap. Snap. Snap. Like twigs. White light assaults us when we enter the bowling alley. We stop, adjust our eyes, and look around. The place is packed because leagues are playing, people with big bellies drinking beer, shouting, applauding their teammates, balls thundering on wood, pins crashing. We walk toward the video games and pinball machines, a corner of the alley protected by glass walls, into the sound of pings and bells and buzzes. Before the entrance, there's a door leading to the

111

lounge, music coming from it, a country crooner:

You picked a fine time to leave me, Lucille

Gilbert spots him playing that video tennis game, Pong. The Filipino kid is dressed in baggy pants and a white T-shirt, *cholo*-style like us; and, as if he knew what was about to happen to him, he nervously looks over his shoulder, although he doesn't see us.

"We can do it here," says Gilbert, pushing his metal-framed glasses up his long, thin nose and looking around. "We'll do it fast, then run."

"Then we'd never be able to come back," I say like the voice of reason; but really I'm thinking this: talking with Johnny de la Rosa's girl, a white girl named Debbie, may not be enough of a crime to warrant what will happen. David Romero told us about it. The Filipinos were hanging in front of the high school, in their regular spot underneath the shade of the big elm tree, about five of their lowriders parked along the curb. Their music was loud, the same kind we Chicanos listen to, Santana, Slave, Diana Ross. Kurt was talking to Johnny's girl as he sat on the hood of a fixed-up '63 Impala. Debbie, we know, likes low-riders. She stayed talking with him all afternoon, as if she were his girl. She took a couple of drags from his cigarette. David Romero held up two fingers and then slapped the palm of his other hand with them. "He boned her, Johnny," he said. And he slapped again. "Boned her."

Johnny looked up at the sky, his eyes filled with sun, and he slowly rubbed his goatee with a finger. He has long hair in a ponytail, and wears a red bandana. "How do you know that?" he asked David.

"Shit, come on."

Kurt, the Filipino kid, is one of the first kids I met when I moved to Livermore. Perhaps we were attracted to each other across the classroom because we were both brown, the only brown. Although we didn't talk much, we walked around together during lunch time, watching other kids play, as if we were both outsiders. One time he invited me to his house, a run-down duplex where he lived with his mother. She greeted me wearing a worn white nurse's uniform, only she wasn't a nurse. She was an assistant who cleaned beds, bedpans, bedridden old men. Despite how tired her eyes seemed, heavy and wrinkled, she smiled, tried to make me feel at home. She offered *pancita* and *lumpia.*

As he sat next to me on the couch with a photo album on his lap, Kurt told me about his big brother who was in the army, how he longed for his return because then things would be good for him and his mom. He showed me a picture of him in uniform, leaning against his lowrider. He was dark as earth.

Now Gilbert says, "I want to get him good. Slow and good."

"Yeah," Johnny agrees.

"We should wait," I say. "Outside."

A skinny Filipino man comes out of the lounge, one of the league bowlers wearing a red pullover, the sponsor's name across the back in black letters: Tri Valley Auto Parts. He comes up behind Kurt. He's perhaps in his late twenties or early thirties, but already bald on top. Kurt jumps at his touch. He pats Kurt on the back and laughs. He says something to Kurt and walks to the bathroom.

"There's no telling who he'll walk out with," says Johnny, peering around beneath the red bandana tied around his forehead. "There's got to be another way." He pinches at his goatee.

"Besides, it's getting late," I say. "If he's with some adults they'll probably leave at eleven when the alley closes." I look at the clock over the bowling lanes, a large, lit up round face with the Coca Cola logo. "It's eight-thirty-seven. That means we'd have to wait . . . uh." I begin to count on my fingers.

"One hundred forty-three minutes," says Gilbert without a pause. "Too long."

"I have to go home," I say. "I have to be in at nine."

"I have an idea," says Gilbert, overhead lights reflecting in his eyeglasses, where Johnny and I are distorted, like cartoon characters on acid. Gilbert is one of the smartest kids in the ninth grade, even though he doesn't care, even though he laughed at the math teacher when he was asked to join the Math Club. He says that since Kurt and I were once friends, I could get him to go with me outside, some ruse that would make him give up his game. If I could get him out there, Gilbert and Johnny could come out and we could get him, slow and good.

Somewhere inside I am reluctant, but I don't know why or stop to consider it. The boys go outside.

I walk up behind him. His hair is so thin I can see his scalp. I'm right behind him. As he plays the video game, his shoulders swing from side to side, up and down, like a boat tossed on rough waters. He's wearing a lot of cologne. I almost tap him, but instead I put my hands in my pockets. "Hey," I say. He jumps. He looks around to make sure I'm alone. "What's up, Molina?"

"I need to tell you something," I say. "It's important."

"What is it?" he says.

"We can't talk here. Let's go outside."

"What? What is it about?" He looks nervous. Suspicious. I feel like saying, "Never mind," going outside and telling the others that he wouldn't go for it. He saw right through it. They'd believe me.

"It's about your brother," I say.

"What about him?"

"I can't tell you here. Come on," I say. "You can trust me."

"How would you know anything?

"Your mom called me. Come on."

He does. He leaves his game unattended. The little white ball misses the paddle. The machine makes a buzz, a warning sound each time a new serve is unreturned, falls into blackness.

Buzz. Buzz.

He's losing.

We walk underneath the lights, out to the wide, well-lit entrance, between the cars, and stop at the far end of the lot.

"What is it?" he says, nervous about his brother.

Johnny and Gilbert appear out of the darkness. He looks at me. He closes his eyes as if he were giving up the ghost, accepting his cup.

They pummel him with slaps on the head and punches to the face and kicks to the groin and stomach, and when he collapses onto the asphalt, they kick him over and over on the head and shoulders and legs, even though he cries like a child and squirms into a fetal position like a baby. After Johnny stops, Gilbert continues kicking him. Then Gilbert stops, looks at us, smiles, and wipes the sweat from his forehead. He takes a deep breath as if he has been working hard and has paused for rest. Then he goes back to work, kicking Kurt in the head over and over again and again. Oh, how red and wet blood bubbles on the face of a brown boy.

"Kick him," Gilbert yells to me, knowing I haven't touched him. But I've done my part.

How Hot Was Mexicali?

Her family drove there in a brown Ford Van. The van had no air-conditioner or windows in the back, so the children ate chunks of ice and rubbed it on their arms, necks, and faces. The little boy, her brother, looked at her and said *Ah!* as he smeared ice on his bony chest, teasing her that she couldn't rub ice on her chest because she was a girl. She stuck her plump little body between the two front seats and begged her mother to turn the van around and go home so she could stand before the swamp cooler. She didn't care what cousins were in Mexicali or how two years earlier when she had seen them last she played with them and had fun. She missed her friends from home, Teresa Navaro, Sandy Brooks, Karen Sakamoto. And besides, she didn't even know the dead uncle. Her mother, eyes heavy from driving in the heat, said that Mexicans respected the dead, no matter how hot it was. The little girl watched the desert road, wet and wavy at the tip, slithering at and under them. Nothing on the sides of the roads but barbed wire fences, maybe, she thought, to stop folks who want to walk in sand and rock.

The van had no backseats. Her little brother spent most of the trip laying on the van floor, wearing only BVDs that were wet, his eyes wide open, sucking his thumb. The little girl, because she was a little girl, had to keep fully clothed. She sat on pillows, her back against the wall, afraid to sleep because she sensed the dream would not let her come back to her body. She wore a blue and white skirt that came past the knees and a red blouse.

Her mother had designed and dyed them herself, cutting the pattern from a white sheet as wide as a map of the world, her thick fingers

117

awkwardly handling the scissors, trying to be gentle and precise, like a man feeding a baby bird. She had wanted for her daughter a dress like girls wore in Mexico when she herself was a girl, but new dresses from Mexico were too expensive. Now the sweaty fabric clung to the little girl's body, and the way the cotton rubbed against her skin gave her icky goose bumps like a wet handkerchief on a tender face.

After one and a half days, they arrived in Calexico, and it was even hotter. Inside the van felt worse than picking grapes in the hot fields, worse than the metal warehouse where they stored the tools, worse than the bathrooms they had to use, warm wooden shacks, leaning in the sun like tired soldiers. Her big 14-year-old brother, turned around from the passenger's seat and squirted mist at them from a spray bottle. The little girl began to dream. She pictured angels breathing on her with cool, sweet breath. She heard them say, as they led her into a beautiful house with air conditioning, "*¡Aquí estamos!*"

Kids gathered around the van with California plates as it crackled over the gravel driveway. Silently they watched while the woman got out and opened her arms to her sister, a fat woman in a loose dress, who came running from the house, hands over her mouth.

The teenage brother was the one who would open the sliding door of the old, brown van. The Mexicali kids, dark as Africans, wearing only shorts, watched the van, watched that hot metal door slowly open. The creak was painful to the ears. Everyone watched.

What they saw made them gasp. Their cousins, the little girl and her little brother, looked like they had been tortured. They stepped from the van on to the hard, Mexicali dirt. Looked like they had been whipped. Like they had forgotten how to live with the sun.

The little boy, upon seeing his cousins, suddenly became animated and lifted his arms and waved and said hello in English and then in Spanish. But the little girl was woozy. She felt like she would fall down, she felt she needed to sleep for a very long time. The kids laughed as she swayed like a baby tree in the wind.

But the aunt felt for her. She took her hand and said, "Come, *m'ija*." She led her into the house, which was cool and dim like church. She led her into a cold bedroom the size of a tomb and told the little girl, in front of a chest of drawers with a wide mirror, to lift her arms. She pulled the blouse over her head and told the girl to step out of the skirt.

She had sweat so much that the dye from the material painted her body.

Red, white, and blue.

"Now that's funny," said the aunt, looking at the mirror image of the little American girl. She laughed a hearty, Mexican laugh.

Too White

I felt bad for the kid but wanted to laugh at the fat cop, who looked around the scene with his eyes squinted as if he were the greatest detective. His fat cheeks and the front teeth that touched his lower lip made him look like a little kid with a badge and a gun. That afternoon I was alone, having gone in the grocery store to walk the tall aisles of wine and liquor, hoping to have guts enough to stuff a bottle down my baggy pants to share later with my friends, Johnny de la Rosa, David Romero, and Gilbert Sanchez, who were, like me, among the few Chicanos in our town. Usually we walked the Livermore streets together, feeling like giants, strutting past small homes that seemed to barely reach our waists, thinking we were bad. We weren't a gang, but we had thought about giving ourselves a name. Kids our age avoided us.

The crowd was pressed so close that our shoulders touched. Suddenly some kid on a ten-speed bike broke through to the front. His handlebars were raised up like ram's horns. He stopped and rested his elbows on the chrome bars, and his face in the palms of his hands.

"Damn," he said, blue eyes wide. "What happened here?" He looked at me, expecting me to answer.

"Some kid got hit," I said.

"Friend of yours?" he asked.

"Nope."

The poor kid, sobbing softly, his bike mangled out of shape, lay in a fetal position on the asphalt.

"Damn," he said. "I'm glad it wasn't me."

From across the parking lot the ambulance wailed as it swerved its

way through shoppers quickly pushing carts to their cars, and it came
to a stop at the scene. The paramedics jumped out, lay the boy on a
stretcher, and took him away. The kid on the bike and I were still standing after most people had left, and he was staring at the blood spots
where the boy had lain. This kid was my age and had very short hair
and so many pimples on his face that his skin was red and purple. He
wore braces, too, the kind that needed to be strapped around his head.
An ugly kid. Uncool.

The fat cop approached us. "All right, boys," he said, flipping the
page of his note pad and licking the tip of his pen. "What did you see?"

I turned away because I didn't like cops.

"We didn't see anything," the kid said.

"When did you boys get here?" he said, pressing pen to pad, as if
we would provide the clue he needed.

"Just a little while ago," the kid said and turned to me. "Isn't that
right?"

"Yeah, that's right," I said. "We didn't see nothing."

He flipped his pad closed, looked us up and down, and said, "You
boys stay out of trouble."

"Asshole," I said as he waddled away.

The kid laughed. "Hey," he said to me, "you want to go to my
house?"

I didn't even know his name, had never seen him before.

"Sure," I said, "let's go."

The house seemed empty, our voices echoing off the beamed ceil-
ings. The sliding glass doors to the backyard looked out onto a
sparkling pool, which was the shape of the number eight, a diving
board, and a flower garden with blues, reds, and greens. I felt like I was
in a movie.

I followed him down the hallway into his bedroom where he had
his own pinball machine, only slightly smaller than the pool hall kind,
and a stereo system better than the one my family shared. On his walls
hung posters of football stars and rock bands whose names I didn't
know.

But it was what he had on the bedside table that caused me to
pause: money, a few dollar bills and lots of quarters, dimes and nick-

els. I looked at the money, then at him, but his head was under the bed, because he was trying to pull something out. I pictured myself putting the money in my pocket and running out of there, but not just yet.

I didn't even know his name.

He piled a bunch of thin boxes on his bed, Monopoly, Parcheesi, Life, and he said, "You want to play?"

I stayed all afternoon playing Monopoly. When I landed on Park Place, which he not only owned but had placed a hotel on, he jumped off the bed and started dancing, rolling his arms as if he were swimming, then holding his nose, covering his mouth and sinking deeper into water. "Oh yeah!" he yelled before he shook his head, face blurring. When he stopped, his eyes bulged and he said, "I'm the greatest."

That made me laugh.

After he had left his room to get us stuff to eat and drink, I looked at the money on the table. It shined and yelled for me to take it. I had none in my pocket, and no prospects of getting any.

He came back with his arms filled with bags of chips, Hostess cupcakes, and Twinkies, cold cans of Coke, and assorted candies. He threw them on the bed and said, "Take whatever you want."

"Wow. This is like 7-11," I said. "My mom never buys this stuff."

He shoved potato chips into his mouth, his face raised to the ceiling while he laughed. As he was still chewing, he looked at me and said with crumbs flying out of his mouth, "I hope you didn't steal any money while I was gone."

"What the hell you mean by that?" I said.

"I'm winning," he said. "So if suddenly you come out with a hundred thousand dollars and buy all kinds of hotels, I'll be suspicious."

I laughed. "You're okay," I said.

"No, I'm the greatest!" He threw the bag of chips on the bed, stood up and moved his arms back and forth like an Egyptian. "The greatest! The greatest!"

I giggled. "What's your name anyway?" I said.

"That's right. We don't even know that," he said. "I'm Kenny."

"I'm Joey," I said.

"Hey, you like music?"

"Yeah, what do you have?"

"Everything," he said. He jumped from the bed and opened his closet, revealing stacks of record albums as high as our knees.

"Do you have Tower of Power?" I asked.

"Never heard of them," he said.

I named off several other bands that Chicanos like me and my friends listened to, Mary Wells, Earth, Wind and Fire, The Isley Brothers, but each name seemed to leave him more confused. Music could divide, could tell us who we were, who we weren't.

He was too dorky, too uncool. Too white. No one could know about this day. I would deny it ever happened. I looked at the money on the table.

"You decide," I said.

He pulled out an album. "This is my favorite," he said. African-sounding drums beat furiously, and then there were screams and wails. We continued playing while Mick Jagger crooned,

> *Please allow me to introduce myself*

Kenny moved his head to the rhythm of the music as he held the dice in his hand, shaking them like a spiritual rattle, blowing on them for luck.

> *Pleased to meet you*
> *hope you guess my name*

Damn it, I couldn't help it: I liked this kid.

That evening I walked home along shadows of tall trees, past homes with vast lawns, down an avenue lined by a brick wall beyond which were more rich homes, onto another avenue dotted with duplexes and small, sagging houses, past Johnny de La Rosa's place. One of his older brothers was working on a car, a naked bulb hanging from the hood, swaying slightly, glowing like a halo. I reached my street-cars on blocks, scrawny, misshapen trees—and went into my home, into my life, where my father, smoking a cigarette, sat shirtless on the couch, stomach flab hanging over his waist. He was watching a boxing match. My mom, at the tiny table in the kitchen, sat before a sewing machine, the whir of the needle a soft sound like an electric razor. "I'm home,"

I announced. They looked at me like I was crazy. As if to say, "And?"

During lunch us Chicanos hung out at the far end of the field, next to the chain-link fence that separated school grounds from the tall wooden fences of people's backyards, me, Johnny de la Rosa, who had long black hair in an Indian braid and wore a red bandanna, David Romero, and Gilbert Sanchez. We were too cool to be involved in anything that went on in junior high, too cool for junior high.

About fifty feet away, a group of white girls sat in a circle smoking cigarettes. They kept looking back at us.

"Would you ever do a white girl?" David Romero said to anyone. David we called Romeo because he always wore slacks, shiny shoes, and his hair was slicked back.

Adrian, a little dark kid who wasn't cool but liked hanging out with us, said, "I know I wouldn't. No way. How about you, Johnny? Would you? How about you, Joey?"

I took a drag of my cigarette, too cool to answer.

"You don't like girls," David said to Adrian. "So shut the hell up."

"That ain't true. I like girls."

"Yeah, your mama," said Johnny.

"I wouldn't, " said Gilbert Sanchez, the only one of us sitting down, his arms straight in back of him. Gilbert was skinny and he wore glasses, and he seemed from a distance to be a little geeky, but up close, you could see that his arms were long and thick with muscles and his face was solid as if chiseled from stone. "I wouldn't want no white girl," he said. His teeth were yellow and crooked.

"I don't know if I would or not," said David Romero. To him the question mattered, because he liked a pretty blonde in our class named Naomi and he wanted our approval to pursue her. "What about you, Joey?" he asked me.

"That's probably all he likes," said Gilbert.

What other options were there? I thought. The Mexican girls in our school were traditional Catholic girls who wouldn't even kiss, or else they were Gilbert's sisters, but nobody was stupid enough to try anything with them.

I looked over at the girls in the circle. "Hell yeah, I would. If she was fine."

"Shit yeah," said Johnny, and he raised his hand to me for the Chicano shake.

"Yeah, me too," said Adrian. "If she was fine."

"Shut up, boy," I said to him. "Why don't you go get us something to eat or something? What did your mama give you for lunch?"

He lifted a brown bag from the ground and looked inside. "I got burritos and some chips."

Gilbert looked at me, cocked his head, squinted his eyes and said, *"Quieres casarte con una gabacha, ¿eh?"*

"Well, uh," I said. "You know. . ."

He slowly shook his head, looking at me. *"No me entiendes, o ¿qué? ¿No eres Mexicano?"*

"Let's go talk to those girls," Johnny said to me.

I watched Gilbert, wondering what he was thinking. His small black eyes quivered behind the glare of his eyeglasses. He had a scar on his chin, as if he had been cut with a knife. Suddenly he perked up, seeing beyond me. "What the hell?" he said.

From the school buildings, where kids played on the blacktop or on monkey bars, a white kid was walking toward us. I knew it was Kenny by the sparkle of his braces in the sun.

"If he comes over here. I'm going to kick his ass," said Gilbert, who was tall and fast and knew karate. He was the best fighter in our group and the one who enjoyed it the most, like dancing he had once said, rhythmic and measured. "I'll kick that white boy's ass," he said.

Kenny got closer, but he stopped and craned his head to get a better look. He was looking for me.

Johnny, fingering his long hair around an ear, said to Adrian, "Friend of yours?"

"That geek? Hell no," said Adrian. "I ain't got no friends like that."

Kenny stood still for a while, and then he turned around, and walked away.

"Boy's lucky," said Gilbert.

Johnny and I went and talked to the white girls.

His mother was a tall, beautiful blonde who looked so elegant picking blue and red flowers from their garden that I was unable to look her in the eyes when Kenny introduced us. "He's a seventh-grader like me," he said, which made me feel small and young, not the way I wanted her to see me.

She stood up, a bouquet in her gloved hands. "Welcome, Joey," she said, and when she smiled at me, I wasn't sure it was the way an adult smiles at a child, but rather the way a woman smiles at a man. She wore navy-blue sneakers and tight nylon pants rolled up at the ankles.

"Kenny, make sure you take out the garbage this afternoon. Tomorrow's garbage day."

"Shit, man!" he said. "I always got to do the slave work around here."

"Just do it," she said, bending over to pick up her hand shovel.

"You do it," he said as she walked away. "I ain't a slave."

"Am *not*," she said.

That afternoon we swam, we played pool on the table they had in the family room, and then we ate sandwiches his mother made, on a long wooden table that shined so much we could see ourselves in the reflection, our faces distorted and cartoonish like in a funhouse mirror. Kenny pulled his mouth wide with his fingers and stuck out his tongue and the mirror image made him look so goofy that I spit milk from my mouth laughing.

I was too embarrassed to have him see my house, so I went to his place a lot, almost everyday, telling my friends that my parents were cracking down, keeping me at home a lot. On weekends his family would do things together. His dad was a lawyer, a thin man who was nice to me and who didn't smoke or cuss or lift his hand to Kenny and tell him to shut the hell up. If anyone did any cursing, it was Kenny, right in front of his parents, and it shocked me that they didn't do a thing about it.

One weekend I went with Kenny's family to the mountains and stayed in a cabin. Kenny and I pretended we were thieves running through the woods with a million dollars in a duffel bag, chased by the police. A bear trap snapped my foot, practically cutting through to the ankle. "I can't keep going," I cried. "Leave me here to die. The money's yours."

"No, we're in this together," he proclaimed. "What's the point of being rich if I can't share it with my very best friend?"

The trees of the forest glittered with sun.

I stood up, suddenly serious, suddenly angry.

"What's wrong?" he said.

My very best friend.

"This is a stupid game," I said.

"It's fun," he said.

"I need a cigarette," I said.

"You don't smoke," he said.

I looked at him standing there, his arms out as if asking why.

He was such a dork.

He was so white.

Too white.

I could see the veins in his neck.

Suddenly we heard rock music coming from beyond a cluster of trees, and we froze. Then, with question marks in our eyes, we looked at each other. Kenny motioned me to follow, and like spies we pushed our way through thickets. In a clearing next to the lake was a Winnebago, and sitting outside of it were two girls, older than us, about sixteen. They sat on lawn chairs in bikinis, one holding a tanning device on her chest like a giant book of mirrors.

"Damn," said Kenny. "Girls."

"Yup," I said. "Them's girls."

"You like girls?" he asked.

"What kind of question is that?"

"Just wondering," he said. "Some guys don't. Some guys think they have cooties."

"You mean kids," I said.

"Yeah, kids, like us."

"I ain't no kid," I said. "I like girls."

One of them, a brunette with her hair in a ponytail, stood up from her chair.

"Damn," he said.

We heard the bell his parents sounded for dinner, so we ran through the woods, the branches of trees and bushes swatting me on the arms and face.

Inside the cabin, we sat around the table, the father, wearing a cardigan sweater, and the mother, in a tight pink blouse with a V-neck, on one side and Kenny and I on the other. There was a plate of hamburger patties with melted cheese, a plate of buns, and another with chopped lettuce and tomatoes. "Dig in, boys," said the father, and Kenny grabbed a bun and put two patties on it. Around his parents I was shy and timid, so I sat there waiting until his mother looked at me with her sky-blue eyes and said, "Go on, Joey. We barbecued them."

"Thank you," I said; and slowly, shyly, I reached for a bun and placed it on my plate. Then I reached for a patty. Kenny started eating, holding his burger to his mouth and chewing happily.

"You kids having fun today?" the father asked.

"We're going swimming after we eat," said Kenny.

"We have to wait," I said. "An hour after we eat or we'll get cramps."

"That's just a myth, Joey," she said. "You can swim whenever you want."

"But my mom said you'll get cramps if you don't wait."

"It's just not true," she said.

The father interrupted: "What does your dad do for a living, Joey?"

"Oh, he's a, he works for the nuclear lab," I said.

"Is he an engineer?" she asked.

"Well, he does, I'm not sure exactly." He was a janitor there. "This hamburger looks great," I said, looking at it sitting on my plate.

"Don't you want lettuce and tomato?" she asked, lifting the plate from the table.

"Oh, no thanks. I just like meat."

"Have you ever been to Disney World?" the father asked.

"You mean Disneyland?" I asked.

"No, I mean Disney World. In Florida."

"I've never been out of California," I said.

"No way! Really? Gosh, I've been everywhere," Kenny said.

"Last year we went to Europe," she said.

"That was boring," Kenny said.

"It was not, you had a great time," she said.

"Well," said the father, smiling and looking at me and Kenny. "We're going to Florida this summer. To Disney World."

"All right!" said Kenny. "It's about time."

"He's been asking us forever," she said to me, and only to me, as if we had a private moment. The hamburger on my plate looked so good.

"Here, Joey," she said, in almost a whisper, her long, thin fingers taking hold of my bun, opening the burger, exposing the meat. Gently she lay another patty on top. It looked stacked, abundant. "If you like meat you should have two patties. A double burger," she said. Then she slid the bun back on. I couldn't wait to bite.

"Thanks," I sheepishly said.

"We'll spend three days at the Disney hotel," the father said.

"Wow, that's neat," I said. "You guys should have fun."

"Would you like to come with us?" the father asked, and then he and she looked at each other and smiled. Then at me. "We know you're Kenny's best friend, and we think he'd have a lot more fun if you were there."

She winked at me.

"You got to come," Kenny said.

"Well, I don't think we can afford it. I mean, I have brother and sister and . . ."

"Oh, you won't have to pay anything," she said. "Kenny would have a lot more fun if you were there."

"I sure would," he said. "In fact, I ain't going without you."

"Kenny," she said, as if he had said something wrong.

Obediently, he said, "I am *not* going without you."

"What do you say?" the father said. "You want to come?"

"Uh, yeah, sure."

"Well then," she said. "I'll call your mommy and get the permission. I look forward to meeting her."

Mommy?

The plate was dark brown, like blood.

"We'll be flying there," said the father.

"On a plane?" I asked.

She laughed, her silver necklace reflecting. "Yes, Joey, on a plane."

"I never been on a plane before."

"This is so cool," said Kenny. Then he turned to me. "Best friends forever," he said, raising his hand for a high five.

His parents were watching, smiling, the father placing his arm around her shoulder. They looked as if they had just done something wonderful and could see the reflection of it in my relationship with their son. My face felt red. I lifted my brown hand. "Forever," I said, feeling the sting of his slap against my palm. They laughed, and everyone started eating again. Except for me. The hamburger looked too big, too much.

"Eat, Joey," she said. "Please eat."

After school, us Chicanos and some white girls were at the park across the street from campus. One girl hung on Johnny and another one was holding on to my arm. Her name was Melody. She looked around as if she thought she were bad, daring anyone who passed the park to look at us. She wore jeans and a halter-top. Gilbert sat on a picnic bench, without a girl, and David on another bench, sweet-talking Naomi.

Johnny said to his girl, "Tell me what people say about me."

"You're baaad," she said.

"What else?"

"Hey, man, when are we going to start our clika?" Gilbert said.

"Let's do it," said Johnny.

"What's a clika?" Melody asked me. She was a pretty girl with a tiny nose and blonde hair.

"That means gang," I said.

"You guys are going to start a gang?" she said.

"Why not?" said Johnny.

"I think that's cool," said Johnny's girl.

"You do?" I asked.

"I'm going to Fresno next week, *ese*, and I got a cousin who's an F14. He could give us some pointers," said Gilbert. "All members have to get jumped in. I know that much."

"What's that?" asked Johnny's girl.

"We all beat the hell out of each new member," he answered. "It's fun."

"What are you going to call yourselves?" said Melody.

Johnny, in a slow Chicano drawl, nodding his head, as if it were the coolest sounding name, ever, said, "The Locos."

"That's a stupid name," said Gilbert. "How about Los Killers?"

We all seemed to notice at once some pale kid on a bike pedaling toward us. My heart jumped because I saw that it was Kenny. Gilbert stood up. I had once seen him throw some guy on the ground and kick him repeatedly in the head. He had a violent streak like none of us had. We just liked being bad, the image, Gilbert liked hurting people. "I just thought of a requirement for the gang," he said. "Kill a white boy."

Kenny stopped his bike in front of us, rested his elbows on the raised handlebars. "Hey, what's happening, fellas?" Then he looked at the girls. "And ladies."

The girls looked at us as if they didn't think he should have the right to be in our presence.

Too slow, too casual, Gilbert walked over. He was going to fly a kick to Kenny's head. Kenny said, "Hi, Joey, you want to go to my house?"

Gilbert looked at me, scandalized, but with a slight smile that said he wasn't really surprised, that he had almost expected it. "This guy's your friend," he said. "This white boy's your buddy."

"Hell no, he ain't," I said. "Get out of here, you little piece of shit," I said to Kenny, stepping between him and Gilbert.

"I got him, Joey," Gilbert called, as if Kenny were a fly ball.

"This one's mine," I said. "Get lost, white boy."

"Bullshit," said Gilbert, "I saw him first."

"What?" Kenny said. He couldn't believe it, didn't recognize me.

"Get out of here," I said, and I pushed him so hard in the chest that his bike fell over and so did he, sprawled on the sidewalk. We all laughed, David, the girls, Johnny, all except for Gilbert, whom I stepped in front of because he was getting ready to kick Kenny.

"Get out of here, you wuss," I told Kenny. In the tone of my voice I heard that I was warning him, protecting him, but that wasn't how it sounded to him.

When he got on his bike he was crying, not because of pain, at least not physical pain. "Get out of here before I kill you!" I yelled. I bit my lip.

He stumbled on his bike and rode away. "To hell with you," he cried. And then he said it again, but in a scream so painful it sounded as if he was falling off a cliff.

To hell with you!

He rode to the end of the park, heading for the exit. His eyes must have been blurry because he crashed into a picnic bench, flying off his bike and landing on the asphalt. We heard the thump. Sobbing. I knew he hurt. He hurt bad.

"Hey, man, what the hell did you do that for?" Gilbert said, stepping up to me. "That white boy was mine."

"Get out of my face," I said, looking Gilbert in the eyes like I was ready to fight.

"You better not be challenging me, punk," he said, stepping in closer.

"Go to hell," I said. "I'll mess you up."

"What did you say?" he whispered, raising his arm, biceps rising, cupping his hand to his ear. "I didn't hear. What did you say?" He came even closer. He pointed at his ear. "I must be deaf or something. I didn't hear what you said."

"I said I'll mess you up."

"That's what I thought," he said, slowly nodding, and then, in a blur of speed his fist came at me. I tried to block but it was too fast and it hit me on the eye like a baseball bat. My eye shut.

I wildly punched back, but all I felt was air.

"Punk," he said over and over as he hit me on the side of the head and on the mouth. "You fight like a white boy," he said.

Blood dripped down my lips. I hurt, but I kept fighting, kept missing, hoping, as Gilbert kept hitting, that Kenny was watching.

Gilbert stopped, as if I had enough. With his arm, he wiped some sweat from his forehead. "You ain't good enough to be in our clika, man. You're too white."

"You punk," I yelled, lunging at him. I grabbed him around the shoulders and pulled him close. I could smell his cologne, his sweat, and for a moment he did nothing, just accepted my embrace, breathed hard, his warm breath on my neck. We moved around in each other's arms, stepping sideways like exhausted boxers, slowly hitting each other in the ear, the side of the head, the mouth.

I pushed him away and punched him hard on the mouth. His glasses fell off, and he looked down at them stunned, surprised. He looked crossed eyed, like a geeky little kid. I hit him again, so hard my fist hurt. He came after me, but I sent two to his face, both of them connecting, causing him to stumble back and then I sent two more to his chest and ribs.

When he bent over, I lunged at him, but he deflected me aside and kicked me in the back of the head, his boot like metal. I fell to the ground, and before I could get up, I felt shadows surround me. Through blurry eyes, I saw three figures standing over me. Then I felt the kicks all over my body, and I heard laughter. Then a siren. The cops were coming. They were all beating me, David, Johnny, Gilbert. I was the first to be jumped in.

Epilogue: Story #7 in D Minor

(The Miracle Night)

What a night this is! It's the kind of night when you can't help but love everyone. The kind of night when nothing can go wrong, that you are destined to enjoy, no matter what happens, no matter what you do; the kind of night that you can find pleasure, even meaning—yes meaning!—in watching a tree blow in the wind, a roach scuttle across the kitchen counter, or by a red wheelbarrow glisten with rain beside the white chickens; the kind of night when you can just sit around the house and do nothing, maybe think about things and people from your past present and future; the kind of night that forces you as you step out on the balcony with a cold bottle of beer to take a good look at life and examine your beliefs and actions, asking yourself the eternal questions, the real biggies, like, "Is there a God?" "Is there a right and wrong?" "Is there something to this not eating meat on Friday?"

Tonight you want to take off your shirt and shoes and defy the rules and walk into the 7-11 and grab a cold Corona from the icebox, rip the cap off with your teeth, gulp down half the bottle, and say to the brown man staring at you with big eyes from behind the counter, "WHAT A NIGHT THIS IS!"

It's that kind of night.

But who am I fooling, reader?

It's a night like any other night.

The End.

Well?

Was there something else you wanted from me, reader?

What?

A story?

A plot that may prove beyond a doubt that the night of which I write is as wonderful as I claim? Maybe you doubt that such a night could be so special—unless something grand occurs. Unless something happens.

Can't I just say it's so, say that I really have no story, just that I feel so good tonight that I have to tell someone about it, and, therefore, the story has ended, go now in peace?

Does it matter to you that on this night I look up and see that the full moon is shining so bright it shoots a white cross into the sky, or that the branches of the eucalyptus trees around my balcony have dazzling spider webs that glow like gossamer wings of light? Isn't that good enough? The night simply is.

But, no! you want to know why this night is so special, as if I had to explain myself to you, as if you wanted to hear a story about how I went crazy maybe, yeah, a story about a crazy *vato*. Got a shotgun and started shooting white people from his balcony across the street from the 7-11 and the university, just started shooting.

Well, I'm sorry to disappoint you, reader, but on this night, this special night, nothing of the sort will take place.

It's just another night.

Well, you're still here.

Hmm . . . .

Maybe I misjudged you, reader. Perhaps you want to know if the voice you're hearing is that of the writer or the protagonist of this story, i.e., Daniel Chacón, unknown writer in despair or a made up character? Well, reader, this is a very good question. But I'm not sure I know the answer.

Okay, here's the story:
It all started when I was born. My name is *Todo Hombre.*

Look, reader, to be honest, I have no story. Although it is me on the balcony this night (tonight!) of which I write, it is not my story I want to tell. I'm boring.
What kind of story do *you* want to read?

How about multiple choice?
I would most like to read a story about . . .

1. A standard identity story about a Chicano boy who doesn't—having lost his chili eating ability—fit in with the Mexicans—they call him *pocho*—and who is rejected as well by the whites—who call him greaser—so he straddles both worlds, unable to figure out who he is, American? Mexican? He's alienated from everyone and cannot connect, so he turns to inner hatred and lives his life confused (and full of rage). He becomes an English teacher at the community college.

2. A magical realist story about a Mexican-American family whose dead grandfather refuses to leave the house. He follows the family members around, dressed in the clothes of a Mexican *revolucionario*, giving his opinion on everything from what they wear to where they go. The family gets so frustrated by him that they consult a *curandera*, who brings the grandfather back to life so the family is once again able to ignore him.

3. A cultural story about an *abuelita* making tortillas on a *comal* while spewing wise *dichos.*

Better yet, *you* write the story!

_____

_____

_____

_____

_____

_____

Well?

Perhaps you don't think I'm being fair enough. Whatever choice you make, whatever you write in the short space provided above, there is still print on these pages that make up words, and these words are arranged by me. It will ultimately be me who will control the story.

Ha! I have you in my clutches!

Realistically, I cannot know what you want to read. Although I am a creator of sorts, I am not The Creator. I will, therefore, have to choose the story myself. Please bear with me, and we will get to the end of these pages as soon as possible.

This is a story about love.

It's a strange story, but not as strange as something that may actually happen in your life or in the lives of the people around you. After all, fiction is strange, but, of course, truth is stranger than fiction.

> Of course, truth is stranger than fiction.
> Of course, truth is stranger than fiction.
> *(Like a deejay:)*
> Of course
> Of course
> course
> truth
> is
> truth is
> stranger than fiction.
> Of course—
> Of course—
> —stranger
> —stranger
> —stranger
> —stra
> —stra
> strangerthanfiction
> strangerthanfiction.
> fic-stran fic-stran fic-stran
> Stranger than fiction.

Fiction, after all, has to make sense.

Okay, okay, the truth is this story took place in old Mexico City, during the transition from Tenochtitlán to Chilangolandia, you know, in the early days. I was never good at history so don't ask for a precise date. Let's just say it was a long time ago. The hero of this story is named Cortez. He was a guy just like me, only he was better looking and exciting things always happened to him. He was young and intelligent and his life's ambition was to marry a widowed woman named Doña Maria, whom he watched every Sunday sitting in the balcony in the cathedral. Unfortunately for our hero, the Doña ignored him, and was, in fact, destined to love another, who happened to be his twin brother, who happened to be a Carmelite monk at a nearby monastery and who, because of his religious vows, happened not to be able to return the Doña's affection.

It's a comedy of errors, I guess you could say. Despite Cortez's repeated attempts to get the woman's attention, he remained unnoticed by her. In such despair, his life started to fall apart. In the middle of a five-day drunk, Cortez promised his Aztec slaves that if he died he would leave everything to them since he had no heirs and since his brother was a monk and had no use for worldly goods. All the Aztecs stood up and smiled greedily, their eyes focusing on Cortez, some of them licking their chops.

"Unless I'm killed violently," Cortez added nervously. "Or if I have an accident."

They sat back down.

"In fact, only if I die by natural causes. And when I'm very very old."

One day neither hot nor cold, our hero said to his monk brother, "Alas! I'm undone! I cannot get the fair Doña Maria to notice me."

"So what?" replied his monk brother. "That's not important. In fact, I told her that when she brought me a cake this morning. I said she should be seeking God, not me."

"She brought you a cake?" replied Cortez jealously, wondering if she would ever bring him a cake, and if she did, would it have sprinkles on it.

"Yes, she often brings me things," said the monk. "Above and beyond her Sunday offering. In fact, tonight she's going to bring me something else. But I gave up such things. You may eat the cake if you like. Otherwise it's just going to collect mold."

"It's not the cake I want, it's her!" cried Cortez. "Don't you understand? I love her so much. Her red lips! Her bright eyes! The way she spits when she says *Huitzilopochtli!*"

"Enough! You are talking rubbish," cried the monk.

"But don't you see, my brother. Nothing is greater than love," Cortez said while he cut himself a piece of cake. "Love is all we have until we die."

"Rubbish!" said the monk. "We have eternity, and cable TV."

Cortez began to eat a piece of cake as he cried.

"You're going to eat that?" said the monk.

"If only she loved me and not you," cried our hero. "Then I would know paradise and what it is to be a man."

"That's not true. Without inner peace you will be miserable no matter what you have. Seek ye first the kingdom of God, and all these things will be given unto you."

"I would give up everything just to hold her once in my arms." And then he added: "And to see her naked."

"Such futile thoughts!" replied the monk. "You should not waste so much time with temporal things. You should be thinking of heaven and hell, and where you belong in God's plan." The monk watched Cortez cut another piece of cake. "You're going to eat the whole thing?"

"Why does she love you and not me? Why couldn't it be me? Why? We are twin brothers. We even look alike."

"Now wait right there, I have dimples when I smile," said the monk, smiling. "Besides," he added, "my skin is much clearer."

"Oh, what I wouldn't give to be in your sandals!"

At this moment an evil thought occurred to Cortez, and no matter how hard he tried to rebuke it, it wouldn't go away.

"I will pray for you, my dear brother, and I guarantee in a fortnight you will be rid of your love jones."

"What's a fortnight?" asked Cortez.

"I'm not really sure. Probably about two pages."

That afternoon, Cortez was walking through the *zócalo* alongside his Aztec friend and loyal servant and slave, Texmexchitli (pronounced TECHS-MECKS-CHEAT-LEE). There were many merchants out that afternoon, many booths made of wood and canvas, people selling rugs and swords and T-Shirts with the Pope on them, and there were food booths, too. Hundreds of people filled the plaza, Spanish people dressed in the stiff clothes of aristocracy and wealth, Aztecs working behind the booths, shoveling beans with big spoons into giant tortillas. Perry the *tamal* monger, who held out two fat tamales in each hand, stood in front of his booth, yelling, "What? You don't like tamales?" to people who passed.

Cortez, our hero, wasn't paying attention to the market as he walked. He watched the only cloud in the blue sky, a small cloud, perfectly round and soft looking. He suddenly wanted to cry.

"Woe is me!"

Texmexchitli wasn't listening, but was staring at a beautiful Aztec girl selling T-shirts to some Spaniards. "Yeah, that's nice, *jefe*," he said.

"Texmexchitli the Aztec, my friend and servant, I must solicit your advice on a certain matter *de la couer*."

"*¿De la qué?*"

"I just cannot get the Doña out of my mind," he said.

"Yeah, that's great. *Pero*, can I borrow a couple of *pesos* for a T-shirt, *jefe*?"

"Texmexchitli, if you do not quit your flirting and listen to me, I swear I'll have your head on a platter!"

"Oh, are we in one of our let's-oppress-the-Indian moods? I don't know about you, Cortez, you and the rest of you *pinche* Spaniards."

"Enough, you Indian dog!"

"Indian dog? Oh, that's real subtle, Cortez. You racist European pig."

"Such insolence must be punished," exclaimed our hero.

"Punish this," said the Aztec holding a plume in the palm of his hand. "I got your punishment hanging."

Cortez drew his sword and slew Texmexchitli the Aztec, who had been prone to react like that quite often, ever since he took that Aztec Studies course at the community college.

Cortez, having no friends and no one to talk to, hired another servant that very day. He was, like Texmexchitli, an Aztec, but he claimed not to be, and he didn't speak much of the Aztec language, except for the dirty words or when he went to visit his grandmother on summer trips to Aztlán when he was a child.

"My friend and Servant, Tim," (pronounced TIM) said Cortez, still perplexed by the evil thought that was suddenly not so evil, but was in fact quite clever. "May I ask you a question about something?"

"Why certainly, my better. What is it?"

"It's a question about God."

"Which manifestation?" asked Tim.

"What?"

"The Father, the Son, or the Holy Ghost?"

"All three I guess."

"Proceed, your greatness."

"Do you think God would be mad at me if I pretended to be my twin brother the monk, so that the fair Doña Maria will love me?"

"Well, that all depends. What is your *raison d'etre*?"

"My wha?" Cortez asked.

"Your purpose, my superior. What is your purpose in deceiving her?"

"Love is my purpose."

"Is it Christian love, my lord?"

"She's got a really cute butt."

"You are absolutely right, your Spanish Pigness!"

"What did you say?"

"You are absolutely right, deceiving her is the best thing to do. Yes. You must dress up like the monk your brother and make love to the fair Doña Maria. Except you must be careful of one thing."

"What's that?"

"You must make sure that you eat no meat, for it is Friday and if you do so, surely you will go to where there will be weeping and gnashing of teeth."

Cortez marvelled at Tim's knowledge and wisdom, but he still thought of him as a second-class citizen.

"We must find a way to get my brother's garment."

Tim suggested that they wait until that evening when the monk takes his bath in the pond. The monk must walk through town to get to the pond. When they take his clothes, he would be forced to stay in the water lest he walk nude through the public square.

Okay, here I am on my balcony this night (what a night!) drinking a few suds, minding my own business, telling you this story. People pass by on the sidewalk below me. Right now—as I write these very words—two young women, obviously Fresno State students, backpacks slung over their shoulders, are walking. The green and red lights of the 7-11 sign shine in their blonde hair. I see them through the branches of the eucalyptus. One's real skinny. I can hear her voice.

Now they're directly below me.

The skinny one: "I mean it. Yesterday I was fatter than I am today, but still I don't want to go to that party because I'm too fat."

Now there's a guy walking by, a boy in his teens. He's looking at his hair. Oh, my god! His hair might be out of place! He's touching it. Wait . . . Yes! He's pulling out his comb with one hand while he pats his head with the other.

No.

False alarm.

The hair is all right. The comb goes back to the back pocket. But just to make sure, he's going to look up, not to the sky, not to the cosmos, not to the stars or the moon, but to his hair. His world.

He's crossing the street to the 7-11.

Cortez was about to put on his brother's stolen cassock when he started to think that maybe it was more than just a regular garment. Maybe it was composed of a special cloth that only the holy can wear. If normal people put it on, if sinners like him put it on, maybe they burn up or go blind or develop a nasty rash.

"Quickly, my better, remove your clothes," said Tim. "We don't have much time before your brother is through bathing in the tarn."

"The wha?" asked Cortez, hiding his clothes in some nearby bushes, and slipping on the cassock.

Cortez began to plan his plan. He sent Tim to the Doña's *hacienda* to give her the message that the monk wanted to see her at seven o'clock that evening.

That night.

At six fifty-five in his brother's quarters at the monastery, Cortez combed his hair and looked at himself in the mirror, just one more time, just to make sure that he looked like his brother, just to see for himself how incredibly handsome he was. He checked his breath and noticed it still smelled of the fish soup he'd had for lunch. He pulled a mint leaf out of his pocket and chewed on it, just in case he should require fresh breath, just in case he should get lucky.

When Doña Maria finally arrived, Cortez was taken aback by her beauty.

"Doña Maria," he said, almost crying with joy. "Come in, dear lady."

"Cut it with the 'dear lady' stuff, will you? I only have half an hour."

"My dear, what ever are you speaking of?"

"Don't give me the monk shit today," she demanded. "Just tell me what you want."

Cortez thought that Tim had betrayed him and told the Doña Maria of his nefarious plan. His own heart suddenly convicted him of the great sin he had committed.

"Oh, I am an evil man!" he cried out loud.

"No shit, Sherlock," said the Doña. "What do you want today?"

Cortez was completely confused. "I want to speak to you, my child."

"It's your call, *padre*, but the price remains the same," she said, lighting a cigarette. "Sex or no sex."

"You mean, you're a . . . ?"

"Little tired of the pious act? Damn right—and none of that sadistic stuff tonight either."

"But . . . but . . . I love you."

"For five hundred *pesos*," replied Doña Maria. "By the way, you still owe me for that cake I brought you."

The images Cortez held of Doña Maria and his monk brother slipped away from him and shattered on the cold, hard floor, and with it broke an innocent belief that he had had, a simple faith in things that are good, like his brother's piety and his love for the Doña.

He wasn't sure what to believe anymore. He did know one thing: He knew that he must send Doña Maria on her way and never again would he be afflicted by his love for her.

He was about to rebuke the evil temptress, but she began to undress; and he suddenly felt a growing urge to hang around, just a little longer, just to see what might happen, just in case. I'll stop her when she gets to her underwear, he thought, but it wasn't until she stood before him totally naked that he realized he wasn't going to stop her at all. I am such a weak man, he mourned to himself. He held his head down in shame. "I'm bad!"

"What?" she said, panicking. "Isn't that check you wrote me any good?"

Cortez did some serious loving that night. He thought they had been at it for over two hours non-stop, but then he remembered she only had half an hour to spare, and after they had finished, and after he had paid her, she still had enough time to smoke and read the paper and take a nap before announcing she had to leave.

"Here, take this," she said, handing him a flyer. "Tuesday's two-for-one day."

The second she left, a great load of guilt fell on Cortez.

"I'm such a devil!" he wailed.

Upon hearing this, Tim entered the room to comfort him. "Your greatness, are you all right?"

"Life is meaningless!"

"That's not true. You have everything to live for."

"Like what?" asked Cortez.

"Well, uh . . . a dazzling spider web."

"How boring."

"Okay, well, how about a red wheelbarrow?"

"A what? Why would I live for a red wheelbarrow?"

"Well, your greatness, sometimes it's the little things in life that you can depend on the most."

"No way!"

"*¡Sí, buey!*"

"That's the stupidest thing I've ever heard."

"But why are you so distraught, my lord? Why so downcast within you? Did your plan not work?"

"Oh, it worked all right," said Cortez. He told Tim what she had said when they met, what disappointment he felt for his brother and Doña Maria, and then finally he explained, in explicit detail, what she looked like naked.

"Life is meaningless!" Cortez cried.

What a night this is! I'm watching the streets right now. I'm right across from the university and the 7-11 just watching people.

The thing about this place is that it's so normal, Fresno, California, not exactly an exotic location like old Mexico City. Yet even though what lives and breathes below me may not be exotic, it is unique. It's beautiful.

Really.

I see the Hmong man and woman pulling up to the 7-11 in a white van. From the back, they pull out trays of fresh donuts and sandwiches. Fresno has one of the largest Hmong populations in the world, and most of them settled about a mile away from here on the other side of the university. Some could pass for Mexican Indians.

Right now a Vietnamese man and his small son are picking cardboard and glass out of the dumpster behind the 7-11.

There's Larry, the old white man who lives among students, dragging his paralyzed leg to the store to buy cat food.

There's the fat lady in a nurse's uniform. She hangs out by the pay phones in front of the 7-11, pretending she's trying to make an emergency phone call. Right when you walk by, she slams down the phone and says to you, as if you were her last resort, "Will you please help me?" And then she'll try to get some money, small change, any amount. But cash only please.

She's out there now. I see her. Still wearing the nurse's uniform. She's walking up to the guy who doesn't want his hair to blow in the wind, who's coming out of the 7-11 now, holding a Big Gulp, drinking through a straw, ever so conscious of his hair, his eyes still upward.

The lady approaches him. She's saying something. Without removing his eyes from above, he shakes his head "no" and continues walking. It looks like she might follow him. She doesn't.

Now I see a figure on a bicycle coming out of the darkness of the empty campus into the light of the intersection. Perhaps it is a student riding home.

Wait, this person is stopped at the corner. He's waiting for a few cars pulling out of the 7-11. He is an older male, that is, older than most students, riding a beat-up ten speed.

He's in his mid thirties, it looks, and he has a mean look about him, like he's used to the hardness of the streets. He has no backpack or books.

He looks as if he's trying to decide whether he should go to the 7-11. The light is out on my balcony, and I'm sitting on a chair with no legs, so I know he can't see me. I can study him closely. He looks kind of crazy, eyes that blink fast and a head that darts back and forth looking all around as if he's paranoid or possessed.

Oh, shit!

I don't believe this!

Shit! He sees me!

He senses I'm here. He's looking around.

That's it. He spotted me.

"Hey," he says.

He's turning his bike around
riding to below my balcony
looking up at me.
Romeo, oh, Romeo.
Damn!

"How you doing?" he is asking.

"Just fine," I am saying.

His shiny red hair is short, combed back, and parted in the middle. He looks tough, like he has been in a lot of fights. But he looks tired too, perhaps of his life.

"Hey, man, do you know where I can get some weed?" he asks.

This guy's got to be kidding.

"I'm not a cop, really, man. I'm just new in town. Come on, man. I don't know nobody."

He pulls his bike closer. The light from the 7-11 sign shines on his face. I see he has knife scars across one cheek, and some on his arm. He also has a tattoo on his bicep, some Aryan brotherhood symbol. It looks like a prison tattoo.

"Where are you from?" I ask.

"Just got out of prison," he answers.

Well, he's honest.

"What's your name?" I ask.

"Jimmy," he says. "Jimmy Veach."

"Well, Jimmy Veach," I say. "I don't have any marijuana, but you're more than welcome to come up and join me for an ice-cold beer."

"Hey, that's cool," he says.

"No, that's ice-cold."

"Man, that is really cool."

"Come on up. I'm in 222."

When Brother Hector finished taking his bath, he climbed out of the pond, but he couldn't find his clothes. He did find, however, behind some bushes other clothes that someone had left behind. He put them on and headed back to the monastery.

On his way through the *zócalo*, many people greeted him, calling him Cortez. It wasn't until then that Hector realized that the clothes he was wearing belonged to his brother, and that he would, therefore, look exactly like him, except perhaps a bit cuter. Brother Hector felt himself getting hungry, so he stopped at a food stand to grab a bite.

"Do you want me to add this to your account, Cortez?" asked Perry the *tamal* monger.

"Uh, sure," answered the monk, realizing that his brother's credit was so good that he could get just about anything he wanted and not have to worry about paying for it. And even though it was Friday, he could eat meat.

"In fact, make it a *tamal* supreme."

Walking further through the public square, he stopped at a stand where an Aztec family sold arts and crafts to the Spaniards.

"How much for that Quetzalcoatl doll?" he asked the Indian.

"How much would you pay for it, Cortez?"

"I want it. Bill it to me." Hector grabbed the doll and continued his stroll through the square.

"It's one of our most expensive items," the Indian yelled.

"That's fine," said the monk. "Bill it."

Before he could get to the carpet seller where he was going to pick out some Persian rugs for his study, a large ugly man stood before him, cutting off his path.

"Cortez," he said with a raspy voice. "We have business to discuss."

"Who are you?" asked Hector.

"You know very well who I am," said the man.

He was fat and seemed to be short of breath. "Tonight's the night," he said with an evil smile on his face.

"Tonight?" gulped Hector.

"That's right, Cortez," the man said.

The picture was suddenly clear: This man was the devil himself who came to collect the soul of his pitiful, lost brother, who had apparently sold it for success in the export business. People sold their souls to Satan all the time. What if the devil really mistook him for Cortez and took his own holy soul by mistake?

"I'm not Cortez!" he cried like a baby. "I'm his twin brother. I'm a monk!"

"Sure you are," said the man, still smiling, looking down at Hector with a big red nose.

"Really I am," cried Hector.

"Be that as it may," said the man, "We have slaughtered your best cows, prepared one hundred gallons of your best wine, and we have had the finest chefs working around the clock. We are ready for the banquet tonight. Everything's going perfectly, like I assured you it would."

"Banquet?" asked Hector.

"Yes," said the man. "The party tonight will not be easily forgotten. The finest musicians have arrived from France, and the deejay starts spinning mixes at nine sharp."

"Wow."

"And the best part of it is that your brother the Brother does not know a thing."

"Really?"

"I know how much you love him, and you wanted to surprise him with this banquet in his honor. Well, he doesn't know a thing. When you hire Manny the caterer, everything turns out right or your money back. Except for the deposit, of course."

"You're Manny the caterer?"

Brother Hector felt suddenly convicted of his great sin. Not only had he taken advantage of his brother's identity and credit, but he also, worse yet, always looked down on Cortez as an evil man, the black sheep of the family, while he thought of himself as righteous. If he was righteous he would have been willing to suffer eternal damnation for his brother, but the first thing he did was sell him out.

All along it was Cortez who was the better one, whereas he, Hector, was merely more handsome. He realized his great sin of pride and he called out at the top of his voice, "Oh, what an evil man am I!"

"Isn't the check you wrote me any good?" asked Manny the caterer, looking worried.

"Yes, it is good," said Brother Hector. "But tear it up anyway. Come to the monastery tomorrow at noon, and I'll pay you in full. Cash."

"Very well," said Manny, turning to walk away. "Oh, one more thing," he said. "When do you want the keynote speaker to start?"

"Keynote?"

"Yes, we were able to get who you wanted. It wasn't easy, but we got him."

"After dinner," Hector decided.

"Do you ever really take a look at life, Jimmy? Do you ask yourself what it's all about?"

"I wonder about shit."

"Like what shit?"

"You know, shit, why things are, you know, so messed up."

"I wonder if Nietzsche was right about God."

"Who?"

"Nietzsche. German philosopher dude."

"Yeah, them German people are smart. My mom had some German in her. But she was Irish too."

"Your mom's pretty smart?"

"She use to work at the post office."

"Wow."

"Yeah. She worked with a lot of Mexicans there. You're Mexican, ain't you?

"Yup."

"Yeah, you look Mexican. I met a lot in prison."

"In prison?"

"Yeah. Some of them I liked too, but we couldn't be too good a friends in prison because they don't really want that."

"Who don't?"

"The gangs and shit."

"You were in a gang?"

"Sure, everyone is."

"But not anymore?"

"No, I thank the Lord Jesus Christ for that."

"The wha?"

Mexico had never seen a fiesta that can even come close to the *pachanga* that night in the *zócalo*. Everyone was there. Spread throughout the plaza were thousands of people seated at hundreds of long tables covered with white tablecloths and crystal wine goblets. There were Europeans and Indians sitting, eating, drinking, and having a good ol' time. Tim was there with his four children and wife. Texmexchitli was there (he will never really die) with his homeboys. Perry the *tamal* monger was there, as was Manny the caterer.

Also, there was a Chicano boy who was confused and full of rage, a dead *revolucionario* who sat with dignity in his officer's uniform, and an old grandma spewing forth wise *dichos*. There was a blonde girl who thought she was too fat, a boy who cared about his hair, a Vietnamese man with his son, and a Hmong couple.

On a raised platform at the head table sat Brother Hector, Cortez, the Doña Maria, a beggar in a white nurse's uniform, and Jimmy Veach, who turned out to be a pretty nice guy, although kind of weird.

"My brother," said Cortez lifting his wine goblet. "This is a fine banquet."

"Thank you, my brother. I hope everything is pleasing to you."

"Oh, it is very pleasing," said the monk, knowing that he would pay for it himself.

"You must excuse me now," Cortez said to Brother Hector.

Cortez went to the head of the table and clicked his glass with a spoon to get everyone's attention.

"My friends," Cortez said to the crowd. "I am pleased you all could make it."

The people, happy to be there, clapped loudly.

"It is with great honor and privilege," he continued, "that I now present to you a very special guest, someone we all know and love: Tonight's keynote speaker. And the author of this story! DANIEL CHACÓN!"

The people burst into applause as I took my place at the podium. I adjusted the microphone and blew in it just to make sure it was still working.

It was.

Finally, I spoke. "I have only one thing to say," I announced.

The whole town was silent, all their eyes on me. Waiting.

"What a night this is!" I yelled at the top of my lungs.

The crowd went wild.